FADING INTO FOREVER

WHAT REMAINS AFTER GOODBYE

HRISHIKESH KARMAKAR

To the ones who have ever watched a sunset alone,
thinking of someone who once stood beside them under
that same sky.
To those who have whispered "I miss you" into the
silence, hoping the wind would carry their words to the
stars.

This book is for you—for the lovers who lost, the
dreamers who woke up to emptiness, and the souls who
carry grief like a second skin.
It is for those who know that love doesn't always get a
forever, but sometimes... it gives us something even more
powerful—a reason to keep living, even when the one we
loved is no longer here.

To the people who have held a hand that was slipping
away, and still refused to let go.
To those who stayed up all night beside hospital beds,
praying for one more heartbeat, one more smile, one
more miracle.

This is for the broken-hearted who smile through tears,
who gather shattered memories and hold them close like
precious jewels.
It is for the strong ones—the ones who walk through their
days carrying the echo of a laugh, the ghost of a kiss, the
ache of what could have been.

To anyone who's ever had to say goodbye without being
ready...
To those still writing letters to the stars...

This book is yours.

And most of all, this is for her.
For Tarini.
For the love that never faded, even when everything else
did.
For the kind of connection that lives beyond time, illness,
and death.

And for every Ronak who keeps loving,
even in the silence that follows a final breath.

— Hrishikesh Karmakar

Contents

Contents

Contents

Contents

Foreword

Fading Into Forever: What Remains After Goodbye
By Hrishikesh Karmakar
Some books are written with ink.
This one was written with silence, tears, and the pieces of a
heart learning how to break beautifully.
Fading Into Forever was not born out of inspiration, but
out of ache. It came to life in the quiet moments—when the
world had fallen asleep but my memories hadn't. When I
found myself haunted not by ghosts, but by the echo of a voice
that would never speak again.
This story is for anyone who has loved someone so deeply,
so irreversibly, that the world changed shape in their absence.
For those who carry grief not as a wound, but as a
tattoo—etched into their soul, unseen but permanent.
It is a love story, yes. But not the kind that ends in fairy
tale kisses and forever promises. It is a love story that asks:
what if forever wasn't the destination, but the cost? What if
love didn't save you, but stayed behind to teach you how to
survive?
Ronak and Tarini's journey is deeply personal. It is
fragile, flawed, and devastatingly human. You may find parts
of yourself in their laughter, their silence, their longing. And
maybe, just maybe, in their goodbye.
If you have ever lost someone you loved—whether to time,
to distance, to death, or to life itself—this book is for you.
I didn't write this story to give you answers. I wrote it so
you wouldn't feel alone in your questions.
—Hrishikesh Karmakar

Preface

Fading Into Forever: What Remains After Goodbye
By Hrishikesh Karmakar
This book was not planned.
It arrived uninvited—like grief. Like love. Like the kind of
memory that wakes you up at 3 a.m. and refuses to let you
sleep again.
I never meant to tell this story. Not like this. But
sometimes, pain needs a place to go. And sometimes, the only
way to carry someone who is gone is to write them into every
page, every sentence, every breath.
Ronak's voice came to me in fragments. At first, he was
just a man standing alone in the rain. A man who had lost
more than he could hold. But the more I listened, the more I
realized—he was not just a character. He was every one of us
who has ever loved and lost, every soul that has ever stood in
the aftermath of goodbye and asked, what now?
Tarini was harder to write. Not because she was distant,
but because she felt too real. Too close. She reminded me of
people I've known and the versions of love I've had to let go of.
Writing her was like writing a farewell letter I was never
brave enough to send.
This story is fiction. But the emotions are not. They are
raw, untamed, and painfully honest.
I wrote Fading Into Forever not to teach, not to preach,
but to bleed. To unravel. To remember.
If you're holding this book, I thank you—for being willing
to feel deeply, to hurt gently, and to sit with the kind of love
that doesn't always end with staying.
I hope this story breaks something open in you. And I
hope it helps you heal from something you never knew was

still hurting.
With all that remains,
Hrishikesh Karmakar

Acknowledgements

Writing Fading Into Forever has been one of the most challenging and rewarding experiences of my life. This novel is not just a story — it is a piece of my heart, shaped by countless moments of inspiration, doubt, perseverance, and hope. I am profoundly grateful to everyone who has been a part of this journey, whether in small ways or large, visible or unseen.

First and foremost, I want to thank my family. Your unconditional love and patience gave me the space and courage to keep writing even when the nights grew long and the emotions felt overwhelming. Your belief in me, even when I doubted myself, was a guiding light through the darkest chapters of this process. To my parents, thank you for teaching me the value of perseverance and integrity, lessons that breathe through every page of this book.

To my friends — especially those who listened to me pour out my heart, offered words of encouragement, and kept me grounded — your support has been invaluable. You reminded me that I am never alone in this creative journey and that stories, like life, are best shared. Thank you for celebrating the small victories and for standing by me when the weight of grief in this story felt too heavy to carry.

To my readers, both those who have followed my work from the beginning and those discovering this story for the first time: your enthusiasm and connection to Ronak and Tarini's journey inspire me beyond words. Writing for you has been an honor and a privilege. Your messages, reviews, and conversations have fueled my passion and reminded me of the power stories hold to heal and unite.

ACKNOWLEDGEMENTS

I am deeply grateful to my editor, whose keen eye, gentle guidance, and unwavering dedication refined this manuscript into its truest form. Your belief in this story helped me push through moments of uncertainty and shaped the emotional depth that makes this novel what it is. To my beta readers and critique partners, thank you for your honest feedback and thoughtful insights — your perspectives challenged me to grow as a writer and storyteller.

This book would not exist without the quiet inspiration of the cities and places that shaped its mood and tone. The streets, the monsoon rains, the bustling markets, and the silent moments of reflection in unexpected corners all found their way into these pages, becoming characters in their own right.

Lastly, and most importantly, thank you to Tarini and Ronak—though fictional, your story echoes the countless real lives marked by love, loss, and resilience. You taught me that even in tragedy, there is beauty, and even in endings, there is hope for new beginnings.

Fading Into Forever is dedicated to everyone who has loved fiercely, lost deeply, and found the courage to carry on.

May your stories, too, be heard.

With deepest gratitude,

Hrishikesh Karmakar

Prologue

Fading Into Forever: What Remains After Goodbye
By Hrishikesh Karmakar
Some stories don't begin with a hello.
They begin with a goodbye.
I don't remember the first time I fell in love with her.
Maybe it wasn't a moment at all—but a slow unraveling, a quiet becoming. Like autumn turning into winter. Like daylight slipping into dusk. Like grief dressing itself up as memory.
Her name was Tarini.
And she was the kind of girl who made silence feel like music and heartbreak feel like a prayer.
She didn't come into my life like a storm. She came like still water, dangerous in its calm, and somewhere in her eyes—I forgot how to swim.
Now, she's gone.
And I don't know who I am without the echo of her laughter in my bones.
They tell you time heals. That the ache dulls, the memories fade, the nights grow shorter. But no one tells you what to do when healing feels like betrayal—when forgetting even the smallest detail of her feels like losing her all over again.
This is not just a love story.
This is the story of what remains after goodbye.
And if you listen closely, you might still hear her—
—in the spaces between my words.
—in the silences I never meant to keep.
—in the fading light, where her shadow lingers longest.

PROLOGUE

This is the story of how I loved her.
And how I survived her.
—Ronak

Summary

Fading Into Forever: What Remains After Goodbye

Tarini was more than just a whistleblower—she was a fierce spirit, determined to expose the dangerous secrets lurking beneath the surface of a world built on lies. But when her courage costs her life, everything she fought for seems to slip through the cracks of reality. Her death shatters the life of Ronak, the man who loved her deeply, leaving him drowning in a sea of grief, haunted by memories and unanswered questions.

In the silence that follows her loss, Ronak struggles to find meaning in a world that feels colder and emptier without her presence. The pain of losing Tarini is raw and all-consuming, but as time passes, a quiet determination begins to grow inside him. The truth she sacrificed herself for is still out there, buried beneath layers of deception and fear.

When a mysterious figure reaches out with shocking revelations, Ronak's fragile world begins to unravel once more. He learns that Tarini's death may not have been the tragic accident everyone believed. Pieces of a hidden puzzle start to fall into place, revealing a shadowy conspiracy, secret allegiances, and a dangerous game of power far beyond what he imagined. Tarini was living a double life—one filled with secrets she never dared to share.

As Ronak dives deeper into the mystery, he discovers that the fight Tarini started is far from over. He is forced to confront not only the enemies who silenced her but also the ghosts of his own heart. In a world where trust is scarce and betrayal hides in plain sight, Ronak must decide how much he is willing to sacrifice to honor the woman he loved and to uncover the truth she died for.

SUMMARY

Fading Into Forever is a gripping and emotional journey through love and loss, hope and despair, truth and lies. It is a story about the lengths we go to hold on to those we love, and the courage it takes to face the darkness—even when it threatens to consume us all.

Part I

The Rise and Ruin of Love

CHAPTER ONE

NEW BEGINNINGS

The early morning sun spilled softly across the rooftops of Pune, casting long, golden fingers that gently touched the city's narrow streets and bustling bazaars. The air was already warm, carrying the distant hum of waking life—vendors setting up their carts, children laughing on their way to school, and the faint clang of temple bells calling the faithful to morning prayer.

In a modest, aging building on a quiet lane, Ronak slowly opened his eyes. The room was small, barely enough space for his cot, a cluttered desk, and a worn-out wooden chair. The walls were painted a pale cream, now faded and chipped from years of neglect, but to Ronak, it was home—a place filled with the quiet rhythm of family life and countless memories, both bitter and sweet.

He lay there for a moment, listening to the familiar sounds of the morning. His mother's soft humming drifted up from the kitchen, mixing with the faint scent of cardamom chai and freshly cooked poha wafting through the thin walls. His younger sister's excited chatter floated in from the next room as she prepared for school.

But despite the comforting sounds, Ronak's heart was heavy with the weight of unspoken worries. At 22, his life felt like a tightrope walk between the dreams he dared to nurture and the harsh realities that tethered him down.

He turned over and stared at the ceiling fan, its slow, rhythmic rotation mirroring the slow pace of his thoughts. College, part-time work, family expectations, and the endless pressure to succeed gnawed at him every day. His father's quiet disappointment and his mother's hopeful prayers formed a chorus of expectation in the background of his life.

"Ronak beta, get ready soon. Today is important, you know," his mother called up the stairs, her voice warm but edged with urgency.

He pushed off the thin blanket and sat on the edge of the cot, running a hand through his tousled hair. Today was the annual college festival, the one day each year when the campus came alive with color, music, and laughter. For Ronak, it was a rare chance to lose himself in the energy around him, to forget the slow, grinding struggle that otherwise filled his days.

After quickly washing his face and dressing in a simple shirt and jeans, he made his way downstairs. The kitchen was filled with the comforting aromas of spices and cooking, his mother bustling between the stove and the table, where his sister eagerly awaited breakfast.

"Eat up," she urged, placing a plate of warm poha and a glass of steaming chai before him. "You'll need your strength."

Ronak smiled and nodded, grateful for these small moments of care amidst the chaos of life.

Stepping outside, the narrow street was already alive with activity. Vendors shouted their wares—fresh vegetables, fragrant flowers, sizzling samosas. The sun was higher now, its warmth pressing down through the dense city air. Rickshaws and scooters zipped past, their horns blaring in a familiar cacophony.

The ride to college was a blur of faces and sounds. Ronak's mind wandered as he thought about the festival—performances, competitions, the laughter of friends. He was not one to seek the spotlight, but the festival was a place where he could be part of something bigger, a small escape from his worries.

As he reached the college gates, he was greeted by the vibrant chaos of students decorating the grounds. Bright banners fluttered in the breeze, food stalls lined the pathways, and music pulsed from speakers set up around the open courtyard.

Ronak moved through the crowd, his eyes drawn to the stage where rehearsals were underway. It was then that he saw her.

Tarini.

She stood near a group of friends, laughing freely, the sunlight catching the delicate earrings that swayed with her movements. Her kurti, a soft shade of marigold, complemented her radiant smile and the spark in her dark eyes. She seemed to glow with an effortless joy that contrasted sharply with Ronak's usual quiet reserve.

For a moment, the noise and motion around him faded. It was as if the world had contracted to the space between their eyes when they met.

Ronak's heart hammered in his chest, and he felt a sudden, unfamiliar urge to close the distance between them.

"Hi," he said, his voice unsteady but sincere.

Tarini turned toward him, surprise flickering in her gaze before melting into warmth. "Hi," she replied softly, a shy smile touching her lips.

They stood there awkwardly at first, but soon the conversation flowed—tentative questions, shy laughter, shared interests. Tarini spoke about her love for painting, the colors she dreamed of splashing across canvases, the stories she wanted to tell through art. Ronak shared his own quiet dreams of building a life that would make his parents proud and give his sister a better future.

Time slipped by unnoticed as they wandered through the festival together, their footsteps syncing with the beat of music and the murmur of excited voices.

As the sun dipped lower and the campus lights flickered on, Ronak felt something stir deep inside—a fragile, burgeoning hope that perhaps, amidst the chaos and struggle, there was a chance for something beautiful.

But even as the laughter echoed and the night settled softly around them, a shadow lingered at the edges of his heart—the knowledge that life's path was never smooth, and love, especially theirs, would demand sacrifices they had yet to imagine.

CHAPTER TWO

The First Meeting Turns Deeper

The college festival carried on into the cool night, transforming the campus into a kaleidoscope of light, sound, and color. Strings of fairy lights twined around trees and poles, casting a gentle glow over the excited crowd. Music spilled from every corner—soft classical ragas mingled with the beat of contemporary songs, inviting everyone to sway, dance, or simply lose themselves in the moment.

Ronak felt a strange mix of nervousness and exhilaration as he walked beside Tarini, who seemed as radiant in the moonlight as she had been in the afternoon sun. The world around them, with its laughter and chatter, became a blurred backdrop to the quiet bubble they now shared.

"So, painting," Ronak began, breaking the comfortable silence. "It's more than just a hobby for you, isn't it?"

Tarini's eyes lit up with a secret joy. "Yes. When I paint, it's like I'm telling stories only colors can speak. It's a language without words—sometimes louder, sometimes softer—but always honest."

She glanced at him, a spark of something vulnerable shining through her smile. "But it's not something I tell many people. My parents want me to focus on engineering, to have a 'secure' future. Painting feels like a rebellion sometimes."

Ronak nodded, understanding the weight of unspoken expectations. "I know that feeling. My family wants me to get a steady job, provide for them, be practical. Dreams sometimes feel like luxuries we can't afford."

They moved slowly past the food stalls, the aroma of spices and sizzling snacks tempting them but neither reaching for anything. Instead, their footsteps brought them to a quiet corner beneath a towering gulmohar tree. Its fiery red blossoms looked like tiny flames against the dark night sky, illuminated by the soft glow of hanging lanterns.

Ronak found himself drawn to that stillness, as if the world had paused just for them.

"Tell me more about your paintings," he said, his voice low and sincere.

Tarini smiled wistfully. "I paint what I feel, not always what I see. Sometimes it's happiness—a burst of yellow or orange. Sometimes it's sadness—a wash of blues and greys. I don't always know what the picture will be until it's done."

She reached into her bag and pulled out her phone, scrolling through pictures of her artwork. Vivid splashes of color, abstract shapes, faces half-hidden in shadows—each piece told a story. Ronak was mesmerized by the passion and emotion in every stroke.

"That's incredible," he said softly. "You've got a gift."

Tarini shook her head, brushing a stray lock of hair behind her ear. "I'm not sure if it's a gift or just a way to stay sane in a world that feels too loud sometimes."

Ronak felt a pang in his chest. Here was someone who, like him, carried silent burdens beneath her bright smile.

They spoke for hours, their conversation weaving between hopes, fears, and memories. Tarini talked about her childhood in a small town, the carefree days spent running barefoot in fields, and the secret dreams she kept locked away. Ronak shared stories of his family's sacrifices, his father's quiet pride, and his own struggles to balance dreams with duty.

At one point, Tarini's eyes softened as she asked, "What's the hardest part about all this for you?"

Ronak paused, considering. "Sometimes, it feels like I'm being pulled in every direction—toward what I want and what I have to do. I worry about failing those I love."

She reached out, her hand brushing his arm gently. "You're not alone in that."

A warmth spread through Ronak, a feeling he hadn't experienced in a long time—connection, understanding, and the fragile bloom of something more.

As the night deepened and the festival lights began to flicker with the approaching hour, they realized hours had passed. Neither wanted the night to end.

"Can I see you again?" Ronak asked, voice hopeful.

Tarini's smile was soft but sure. "I'd like that."

They exchanged numbers, the promise of future meetings lingering between them like a delicate thread of hope.

Walking away, Ronak felt lighter, as if a weight had lifted from his shoulders. The world still held its struggles, but tonight, for the first time in a long time, he believed in the possibility of happiness.

Underneath the vast, star-studded sky, two souls had quietly begun to intertwine—unaware yet of the storms and joys that awaited them.

CHAPTER THREE

THE FIRST PROMISE

The days after the festival were filled with a strange, beautiful kind of anticipation. Ronak's routine—once monotonous and heavy—now carried a new rhythm, set by the gentle ping of his phone signaling a message from Tarini. Each word she sent was like a small spark lighting up the dark corners of his mind.

Their conversations grew longer, stretching from hurried good mornings to quiet late-night chats about dreams and doubts. It was in these moments, behind the screens, that Ronak saw sides of Tarini no one else did—the tender fears she hid, the fierce hope she clung to, and the raw honesty that made her so real.

One day, Tarini suggested meeting again—not at the noisy college festival, but somewhere quiet, somewhere they could truly talk. She picked a small, cozy café nestled near the riverbank, a place she said felt peaceful and full of memories.

When Ronak arrived, the sun was dipping low, casting warm golden hues over the water and the old brick walls of the café. Tarini was already there, seated by the window with a soft smile, the late afternoon light playing in her hair like threads of gold.

"Hi," she said simply, her voice a melody that made Ronak's heart thud painfully yet beautifully in his chest.

"Hi," he replied, almost breathless, sitting down across from her.

They ordered chai and samosas, the aroma mingling with the scent of wet earth and blooming jasmine outside. The café was quiet except for the soft murmur of other patrons and the occasional clink of cups.

For a long while, they talked about everything and nothing. Tarini spoke about her childhood in a small town far from the city's noise—days spent running barefoot in the monsoon rains, the smell of wet soil after the first storm, the simple joys she remembered with a wistful smile.

Ronak shared stories of his own family—the silent sacrifices his parents made, the dreams he carried not just for himself, but for his sister and the life he hoped to build for them.

The conversation deepened, turning toward their fears—the kind no one spoke aloud. Ronak admitted how he sometimes felt crushed beneath the weight of expectations, how the future seemed a vast, dark ocean he wasn't sure he could navigate.

Tarini's gaze softened, her fingers brushing his hand across the table. "Do you ever feel scared?" she asked quietly. "About what lies ahead?"

"Every day," Ronak said honestly. "But I think it's the fear of losing what matters that makes everything feel so fragile... and precious."

Tarini nodded, a tear glimmering in her eye that she quickly wiped away. "I'm scared too. About being misunderstood, about dreams slipping through my fingers. But I also believe that sometimes, fear is just the price we pay for loving something real."

Ronak looked at her, feeling the full weight of her words, the courage it took to admit vulnerability. He reached out, his fingers closing gently around hers, grounding himself in the warmth of her touch.

"I want to be real with you," he whispered. "No more hiding behind walls, no more pretending. I want us to be honest, even when it's hard."

Tarini smiled through the tears, squeezing his hand in return. "I want that too."

They sat together as the sun slipped below the horizon, the sky painted in deep shades of purple and orange. Around them, the world moved on, but in that small café by the river, time felt suspended—two souls quietly promising to be each other's strength, to face whatever came together.

Yet, beneath the beauty of that promise lay an unspoken truth: the fragility of hope in a world where love often comes with pain.

As they walked out into the cooling night, their hands still entwined, neither could foresee the storms that awaited them, nor how that first promise would be tested.

THREADS OF TRUST

The days after their riverside meeting unfolded like the slow, delicate bloom of a rare flower—each moment layered with cautious hope and the tentative weaving of trust between two souls craving connection.

Morning light filtered through the curtains of Ronak's small room, painting soft golden streaks across his worn-out textbooks and scattered notebooks. His phone buzzed quietly on the table. He reached out with a smile before even opening his eyes—there was Tarini's message waiting for him:

"Good morning, Ronak. I hope today brings you a reason to smile."

That simple message, tender and sincere, felt like a balm for his tired spirit. His fingers hovered over the keyboard for a moment before he typed back, *"Good morning, Tarini. You already gave me a reason."*

It became their ritual—an exchange of words, little moments of light in the daily grind of classes, part-time jobs, and family responsibilities. These messages were more than mere texts; they were lifelines. Each word carried warmth, connection, and an unspoken promise that neither was truly alone.

When they met in person, it was as if the world around them softened. The chaotic campus, the judgmental eyes, and the crushing pressure of future expectations faded to the background. They found refuge in quiet corners of the city—forgotten bookshops filled with the scent of aged paper, parks where they could sit beneath ancient trees and talk about anything and everything, and street-side stalls that served steaming chai and spicy snacks.

One Saturday, the monsoon clouds hung low and heavy, the air thick with the scent of wet earth. Ronak waited under the sprawling canopy of an old banyan tree by the riverbank, its roots twisting like silent sentinels around him. The sky threatened rain, and a soft drizzle began, blurring the edges of the city and the river.

When Tarini arrived, her dark hair damp from the rain, her eyes shone with a mix of excitement and vulnerability. She held tightly to a small sketchbook, its cover worn from frequent use.

"Look what I brought," she said softly, opening the book to reveal pages bursting with color—sketches of the river in different moods, trees bending with the wind, faces of strangers they had passed but never spoken to.

Ronak's breath caught. Each stroke of her pencil and brush told a story deeper than words could express. The colors weren't always bright; some pages were dark and heavy, shades of blues and greys that spoke of nights filled with worry and dreams weighed down by doubt.

"You see the world differently," Ronak murmured. "Through your eyes, everything becomes alive in a way I never noticed before."

Tarini's smile was shy but proud. "It's how I try to make sense of the chaos. When words fail, art speaks."

She flipped to a page filled with swirling reds and oranges—a fiery storm of emotion. "Sometimes, it's anger. Sometimes it's hope. Sometimes it's just me trying to hold on."

Ronak traced the edge of the page gently. "I want to understand all of it. Every color, every story."

Tarini's hand found his, fingers curling around his in a touch both grounding and fragile.

"Maybe," she whispered, "we can be each other's refuge. The kind of safety we both need."

Ronak looked into her eyes and felt a surge of something fierce and tender. "I want that too. No matter what comes, I want us to hold on to this—our truth, our promise."

They sat there for a long time, the rain pattering softly around them, the river murmuring secrets beneath the swollen clouds.

But even in the warmth of their growing bond, shadows lingered. Ronak knew that outside this moment, the world was harsh and unyielding. Family demands pressed on him—his father's tired face, the expectations he carried like a stone in his chest. Tarini's dreams too were fragile, trapped between her passion and the practical path her parents insisted she follow.

At night, Ronak lay awake, haunted by worries. What if their worlds—so different yet so entwined—pulled them apart? What if the dreams they dared to share with each other slipped away like water through fingers?

Yet, when he thought of Tarini's smile, the way her eyes lit up when she spoke about her art, the gentle touch of her hand in his, a fierce determination grew inside him.

They were two fragile flames, flickering against the storm—but together, they might just be strong enough to survive.

CHAPTER FIVE

WHEN WALLS BEGIN TO FALL

The late afternoon sun hung low over the city, casting long golden shadows through the sprawling branches of the ancient mango trees lining the university garden. The air was heavy with the scent of jasmine and damp earth, the soft hum of cicadas blending with distant voices echoing from classrooms. It was a place that felt suspended between worlds—a quiet refuge from the demands and noise of everyday life.

Ronak arrived early, his heart beating with a strange mix of anticipation and unease. He had known for days that this meeting was important, but the words he wanted to say tangled in his throat like thorny vines. As he walked toward the familiar stone bench where Tarini waited, clutching her ever-present sketchbook, he wondered if she too felt the weight of what was about to unfold.

Tarini looked up as he approached, a hesitant smile playing on her lips but her eyes clouded with something heavier—an unspoken worry, a vulnerability that made Ronak's chest tighten.

"Hey," he said gently, sitting down beside her. The rough stone was cool beneath his hands, a grounding contrast to the warmth of her presence.

"Hey," she whispered back, her voice fragile.

The two sat side by side, the quiet between them thick with things left unsaid. Ronak could see the faint trembling of Tarini's fingers as they toyed nervously with the corner of her sketchbook.

"I've been thinking a lot," she finally began, her gaze fixed somewhere beyond the trees, lost in shadows and memories. "About what I want... and what everyone expects from me."

Ronak waited, his silence an open invitation.

Her voice cracked as she continued. "My parents want me to be practical. To choose a future that's safe, steady. Engineering, medicine—things that make sense to them. But my heart... it belongs to my art. To the colors, the shapes, the emotions I pour into every sketch."

She closed her eyes briefly, swallowing hard. "I feel like I'm caught between two worlds—one where I'm supposed to be someone I'm not, and another where I'm afraid to be fully seen."

Ronak reached out, gently taking her hand in his. "You don't have to be afraid with me," he said softly. "I see you—every part of you. And it's beautiful."

Tears welled up in Tarini's eyes, glistening like morning dew. "Sometimes, I think I'm drowning under the weight of expectations. Like no matter how hard I try, I'm never enough."

Ronak's heart ached at her words. He had felt that crushing pressure too—the silent demands of family, society, and self. "I know that feeling," he admitted. "But you're not alone in this. I'm here. We'll find a way

together."
Their fingers intertwined, a simple touch anchoring them in a moment that was both fragile and fierce.

Tarini's eyes met his, searching for hope in the depths of his gaze. "How do you keep going, even when the road seems impossible?"

Ronak smiled softly, though his own fears lingered in the shadows. "Because I believe in the people I love. Because I believe in us. And sometimes, that's enough to keep fighting."

They talked long into the evening, sharing dreams they had never voiced aloud and fears they'd hidden behind smiles. Walls crumbled in the safety of each other's presence, revealing raw, aching truths.

As twilight descended and the first stars blinked awake, Ronak pulled Tarini close, his arms a shield against the world's harshness. She rested her head on his shoulder, finding strength in the steady beat of his heart.

In that quiet embrace, they made a silent vow—not just to face the battles ahead, but to hold each other's broken pieces with care and love.

Yet even as their hearts entwined, an unspoken shadow lingered—a hint of the tragedy that fate had already begun to weave into their story.

CHAPTER SIX

FRACTURES BENEATH THE SURFACE

The weeks that followed were like the slow, grinding turning of a heavy millstone—each day pressing down with relentless weight, grinding away the edges of innocence and hope. The world around Ronak and Tarini, once filled with quiet beauty and shared dreams, was now laced with tension, worry, and silent battles no one else could see.

Ronak's mornings began earlier, waking before dawn to help his mother with chores before rushing off to college. His father's tired eyes watched him quietly over breakfast, the unspoken disappointment thickening the air like a dense fog. His father never voiced it aloud, but Ronak could feel it—the pressure to succeed, to be the man who would carry the family's future on his shoulders.

At college, Ronak kept his head down, burying himself in textbooks and assignments, but the ache of responsibility was a constant weight on his chest. The rare moments he could steal to meet Tarini became lifelines, breaths of fresh air amid the suffocating expectations.

Tarini's world was no less heavy. Her parents, who had once indulged her love for art with soft smiles and gentle encouragement, had begun to withdraw. Their words had grown sharp and impatient.

"Art won't feed you," her mother told her one evening, her voice taut with worry and frustration. "You need a stable future. Engineering or medicine—something that makes sense."

Tarini sat silently, the words hitting her like stones. Her father, usually quiet, nodded in agreement, his eyes filled with a tired resignation.

In her small room, surrounded by sketches and paintbrushes, Tarini felt her dreams slipping away like grains of sand through her fingers. Each attempt to reconcile her passion with her family's demands left her more fractured, more lost.

One evening, Ronak found her sitting by the window of the university library, her sketchbook open but her gaze distant. The dim light cast soft shadows over her face, revealing the exhaustion and worry she tried so hard to hide.

"Tarini," Ronak said softly, sliding into the seat beside her.

She looked up, eyes meeting his with a flicker of relief and pain. "I'm tired, Ronak. So tired."

He reached out, his hand warm against hers. "You don't have to carry it alone."

She sighed, voice breaking. "Sometimes I feel like I'm drowning—caught between what I love and what I'm expected to be. And I'm scared, Ronak. Scared that I'll lose myself trying to be what they want."

Ronak's throat tightened. "I'm scared too. But we have each other. We can be the strength when the world feels like it's breaking us."

Tarini nodded, but tears slipped down her cheeks. "I don't want to be a burden."

"You're not a burden," Ronak whispered. "You're everything to me."

They stayed like that for hours, sharing the weight of their fears and hopes. It was in these moments—broken, raw, and honest—that their bond deepened beyond words.

Yet, even as they clung to each other, the fractures beneath the surface grew wider. The pressures from their families, the harsh realities of their worlds, and the silent shadows of doubt threatened to pull them apart.

Ronak's nights were restless, haunted by the thought of losing Tarini—not just to the world's demands but to the despair that sometimes shadowed her eyes. He found himself promising silently to protect her, to fight for their love even when it seemed impossible.

One rainy night, as thunder rumbled softly outside his window, Ronak wrote in his journal:

"Love is not enough—not when the world is this cruel. But it is the only thing I have to hold onto. For Tarini. For us. I will not let go."

The storm outside mirrored the storm within—a battle of hope and fear, strength and vulnerability.

CHAPTER SEVEN

THE WEIGHT OF SILENCE

The late summer afternoons in the city were filled with a golden haze, soft and almost dreamlike. The kind of light that filtered through dusty windows, casting warm, lazy shadows on cracked walls. But inside Ronak's small home, the atmosphere was heavy — thick with things left unsaid, with fears and hopes tangled in a web of silence.

For weeks now, Ronak had felt a subtle shift in Tarini's presence. The easy laughter they once shared was quieter, more guarded. The way her eyes would sometimes glaze over when she thought no one was watching, as if the weight of the world pressed down on her too heavily to carry.

He wanted to reach out, to pull her close and tell her everything would be alright — but something held him back. A quiet worry that maybe, just maybe, she was slipping away in ways he didn't yet understand.

One evening, after a long day of classes and part-time work, Ronak found Tarini sitting alone on the rooftop terrace of his house. The city sprawled out below them, alive with twinkling lights and distant sounds. The air was cooler now, carrying the faint scent of jasmine from the garden below.

She sat curled against the low wall, her sketchbook closed on her lap, eyes fixed on the horizon where the sun was melting into the skyline.

"Tarini," Ronak said softly as he approached. "I've been worried about you."

She didn't turn at first. The silence stretched between them, fragile as glass.

Finally, she spoke, her voice a bare whisper. "It feels like everything is closing in on me, Ronak. My parents... their expectations, the pressure to give up what I love. Sometimes it feels like I'm suffocating, like the colors I paint with are fading."

Ronak sat beside her, his heart aching. "I know it's hard. I feel it too — the weight of what we have to be, not who we really are."

She swallowed hard, her fingers tightening around her sketchbook. "But what if it's too much? What if loving each other isn't enough to save us?"

Ronak reached out, gently brushing a stray hair from her face. "Love is what keeps me going, Tarini. But I know it can't fix everything. We have to be strong together."

Tears finally spilled down her cheeks, glistening in the fading light. "I'm scared, Ronak. Scared that one day I'll have to choose between my dreams and the people I love."

He held her close, whispering, "Then we'll fight for those dreams. Together."

That night, alone in his room, Ronak stared at the ceiling, thoughts swirling like a storm.

How do I protect her from the world? How do I protect her from losing herself?

He wanted to believe their love was a fortress — unbreakable, unwavering. But the truth was, even the strongest walls could crumble under relentless pressure.

Meanwhile, Tarini lay awake in her small room, the walls lined with sketches that once brought her joy now seeming to mock her. She traced the edges of a drawing, a swirling tempest of reds and blues, reflecting the chaos inside her heart.

Her phone buzzed with a message from Ronak:

"No matter what, I'm here. We'll face everything together."

A fragile hope flickered inside her, but it was accompanied by a deep, gnawing fear — the fear of loss, of being torn apart by forces beyond their control.

In the days that followed, their moments together grew both more precious and more painful. They laughed, they cried, and sometimes they just held each other silently, knowing words weren't enough.

But the silence that stretched between their conversations was growing — a quiet fracture that neither dared to confront fully.

One afternoon, after a particularly harsh argument with her parents, Tarini returned to Ronak's side with a hollow look in her eyes.

"I don't know how much longer I can keep pretending," she whispered.

Ronak tightened his grip on her hand, voice steady despite the storm inside him. "You don't have to pretend with me. We'll find a way. I promise."

But even as he spoke, a cold shadow crept into his heart — a warning that the battles ahead might demand more than they could give.

CHAPTER EIGHT

SHATTERED DREAMS AND QUIET PROMISES

The cool breath of early autumn swept through the narrow lanes of their neighborhood, mingling with the earthy scent left behind by the monsoon rains. Outside, the city was slowly shedding its summer heat, the sky turning a crisp shade of twilight blue. But inside Tarini's small room, the atmosphere was thick with unspoken fears and the weight of dreams slipping through trembling fingers.

For days, Tarini had been battling a growing storm inside herself—one she barely understood, but which dragged her deeper into shadows she could no longer ignore. The sketches she once poured her soul into lay abandoned on her desk, colors muted, lines fractured like her resolve.

Ronak had noticed the change the moment he walked into the quiet apartment that evening. Tarini sat by the window, the fading light painting soft halos around her face, but the spark in her eyes had dimmed, replaced by a hollow tiredness.

"Tarini..." he said gently, approaching her slowly so as not to startle. "You've been distant lately. What's going on?"

She turned, her gaze meeting his, and for a moment, the vulnerability she tried so hard to hide spilled forth. "I'm scared, Ronak. Scared I'm losing myself, that the dreams I've held onto are slipping away."

Ronak reached out, taking her hands in his. "I'm here. Whatever happens, I'm with you."

Tears welled up in her eyes as she leaned into his warmth. "Sometimes I wonder if loving each other is enough. If we can survive this pressure—from our families, from life itself."

Ronak's heart clenched at her words. "Love isn't magic. But it's the only thing strong enough to keep us fighting. We have to believe that."

She nodded, but the ache behind her smile was unmistakable.

Over the following days, their stolen moments together became lifelines—quiet evenings sharing dreams beneath the stars, whispered promises in the dark, and fragile hopes that tomorrow might be kinder.

But reality's grip only tightened. Tarini's parents grew more insistent, their voices sharp with disappointment and fear. "Art won't build a future, Tarini," her father said one evening, his hands clenched into fists. "You need to think about your life."

Her mother's eyes brimmed with tears, caught between love and the harsh demands of survival. "Please, think of what's practical."

Each confrontation left Tarini more shattered, retreating further into herself.

Ronak stood by her side, fighting his own battles at home—the burden of being the son expected to be the pillar of strength, the one to bring hope to a struggling family.

One night, unable to bear the silence any longer, Ronak took Tarini's hand and led her to the rooftop beneath the sprawling sky.

"Look," he whispered, pointing toward the stars beginning to twinkle in the deepening blue. "No matter how dark it gets, there are still lights shining. We have to hold onto those."

Tarini squeezed his hand, a tear tracing a path down her cheek. "I want to believe, Ronak. I want to hold on."

They stayed there for hours, wrapped in each other's arms, a fragile sanctuary from the storm raging around them.

Yet beneath their love, a quiet truth lingered—the bitter knowledge that sometimes, even the deepest love cannot shield from life's cruelest turns.

CHAPTER NINE

ECHOES OF BROKEN PROMISES

The monsoon rains had finally softened, leaving behind a city drenched and glistening under the early autumn sun. Streets sparkled with puddles reflecting fractured fragments of life, just like the fragile state of Ronak and Tarini's world. Though the city pulsed with its usual energy — rickshaws honking, street vendors calling, and children laughing — inside their hearts, a storm raged quietly, relentless and unforgiving.

Ronak's footsteps echoed on the uneven pavement as he wandered through the crowded market lanes alone, lost among faces and colors that blurred past like ghosts. His mind was a tempest of worry and doubt. Every thought led back to Tarini — the girl whose smile once lit up his darkest days, now veiled behind a curtain of exhaustion and despair.

Her laughter, once a melody that lifted his spirits, had grown scarce. The sparkle in her eyes dimmed, replaced by shadows he feared were growing deeper each day.

He clenched his fists, biting back the helplessness clawing at his chest. How could he reach her when she was slipping away into silence?

Meanwhile, Tarini sat alone in her small apartment, the faint light of a desk lamp casting long shadows on the walls. Her hands trembled as she held her sketchbook, its pages worn and heavy with the weight of her emotions.

Each stroke she made was a silent cry — a desperate attempt to pour her pain and confusion into something tangible, something real.

Her parents' words echoed in her mind, harsh and unforgiving. "Art won't build a future," her father had said coldly just days before. "You need to be practical. You need security."

Her mother's eyes had filled with tears, caught between love and the harsh reality they faced.

Tarini's chest ached with the burden of these expectations, the pressure squeezing the very breath from her lungs.

That night, Ronak arrived at her doorstep as the city lights flickered on, casting a soft glow on the damp streets. The air was cool, carrying the scent of wet earth and distant jasmine.

When Tarini opened the door, her face was pale, eyes red-rimmed but still shimmering with a fragile hope.

"Ronak," she whispered, stepping aside to let him in. Inside, the small room was cluttered with paints, brushes, and unfinished canvases — the remnants of a dream fighting to survive.

Ronak moved closer, his voice gentle but firm. "I missed you today."

She managed a faint smile, but it didn't quite reach her eyes. "I'm sorry. I didn't mean to shut you out."

"You don't have to apologize," he said, taking her hands in his. "I want to understand. Tell me what's hurting you."

For a long moment, she said nothing, her gaze dropping to the worn floor. Then slowly, she began to unravel the tangled knots of fear and sadness inside her.

"The pressure from my parents is crushing me," she confessed. "They don't see art as a future — just a childish dream. Every day, I feel more alone, more trapped. And I'm scared I'll lose myself trying to be what they want."

Ronak's heart ached at her words, but beneath the pain, a fierce determination rose.

"We'll find a way," he promised, his voice steady and unwavering. "Together. No matter what."

She looked up, meeting his gaze, and for a brief moment, the walls around her heart seemed to soften.

They sat close, fingers entwined, sharing the fragile comfort of their love — a fragile sanctuary amid the chaos of their worlds.

But as the night deepened, so did the weight of the unspoken truth. The question lingered between them like a shadow:

Could love alone be enough to withstand the storms threatening to tear them apart?

Ronak held Tarini's hand tightly, silently vowing to protect her, to fight for their dreams — even when the future seemed uncertain and cruel.

They spoke little after that, knowing words could never fully capture the ache in their souls.

Instead, they clung to each other — fragile, scared, but still holding on.

33

CHAPTER TEN

FRACTURES BENEATH THE SURFACE

The days slipped by like sand through restless fingers—each one more burdensome, more filled with silent battles that neither Ronak nor Tarini fully voiced. Autumn deepened around them, painting the city in hues of gold and melancholy, while the chill in the air seemed to seep not just through their clothes, but deep into their hearts.

At college, Ronak's world was a tightrope walk between endless responsibilities and stolen moments with Tarini. His father's voice echoed in his mind, a constant reminder of the man he was expected to be — practical, strong, unyielding. But Ronak's heart belonged to Tarini, whose own life was unraveling thread by fragile thread.

One late afternoon, Ronak waited outside Tarini's modest building, the sky swirling with bruised purples and fiery oranges as the sun began its slow descent. The streets hummed with the evening rush — the calls of vendors, the chatter of passersby, and the distant roar of traffic.

When Tarini finally appeared, her footsteps slow and hesitant, Ronak's heart clenched. Her face was pale, eyes shadowed by worry. She avoided his gaze, but he gently called her name.

"Tarini," he said softly, stepping closer. "Please, talk to me."

She paused, swallowing hard as if weighing the words trapped inside her. "I don't know how much longer I can keep fighting, Ronak. Everyone wants me to give up — my parents, the world... even myself sometimes."

His hand lifted, fingers brushing a stray lock of hair from her face. "You're not alone," he vowed quietly. "We'll face this together, no matter how hard it gets."

Her eyes shimmered with tears as she whispered, "But what if I break? What if the weight crushes me?"

Ronak's arms wrapped around her tightly. "Then I'll be here to catch you. Always."

That night, they found refuge on the rooftop, beneath a sky thick with stars that seemed distant yet constant. The city's hum softened into a lullaby as they sat pressed close, sharing whispered dreams and unspoken fears.

Ronak traced gentle circles on her back, trying to soothe the tremors beneath her skin. "I wish I could shield you from everything," he admitted.

Tarini's breath hitched. "Sometimes, love feels like the only thing I have left — but also the thing I'm most afraid to lose."

He pulled her tighter. "You won't lose me. Not ever."

Yet beneath the fragile bubble of their love, cracks began to form—subtle, but undeniable. The harsh truths of their families' expectations, financial struggles, and the looming uncertainty of their future pressed relentlessly on their shoulders.

Days later, a harsh argument with Tarini's parents left her shaken and withdrawn, while Ronak faced his own battle with his father's disappointment.

Alone one evening, Ronak stared at a faded photograph of them together — smiling, hopeful — a stark contrast to the uncertainty clouding his heart now.

He knew the road ahead would be brutal. But he also knew one thing with unwavering certainty: he would fight for Tarini, for their love, even if it meant breaking his own limits.

SILENT CRIES AND FRACTURED HEARTS

The city's nightscape stretched beyond Tarini's window, glittering with countless lights that felt cold and distant compared to the warmth she longed for inside her small room. But tonight, the warmth was nowhere to be found.

Tarini lay curled up on her bed, clutching a worn photograph of her and Ronak—edges frayed, colors faded from countless times being held close to her heart. The smile they shared in that captured moment felt like a fragile thread holding together the pieces of her unraveling world.

She closed her eyes and let memories wash over her—the laughter they shared during lazy afternoons in the park, the stolen glances during college, the quiet moments beneath the vast night sky where promises were made without words. Those memories were bittersweet now, like fragile glass—beautiful but dangerously close to shattering.

The weight of the days pressed hard on her chest—the harsh words from her parents still ringing in her ears, the suffocating pressure to give up her art and conform to a future she didn't want. Every expectation chipped away at the dreams she held so tightly.

Her phone buzzed softly on the bedside table, breaking the silence. She reached for it with trembling hands. It was Ronak.

"I'm here. Always."

Tears blurred her vision as she typed back, fingers shaking.

"I'm scared, Ronak. I don't know how to keep going."

Minutes later, a soft knock echoed at her door. Ronak stood there, eyes full of worry, breath catching from the run up the stairs.

Without a word, she threw herself into his arms, sobbing into his chest as he held her close.

"I don't want to lose you," she whispered, voice trembling.

Ronak kissed the top of her head, his own heart breaking. "You won't. I promise. We'll get through this—together."

They sat down on the bed, Ronak brushing away her tears as they talked quietly through the night. She spoke of the fears she'd bottled up—the feeling of being torn between her family's expectations and her own desires, the creeping dread that her dreams might slip forever out of reach.

Ronak shared his own struggles—the pressure to be the strong son, the burden of responsibility weighing him down. Yet, in his voice was unwavering determination.

"No matter what happens, I'll fight for us. For you."

Their hands found each other, fingers intertwining tightly, grounding them in the fragile present.
Though the dawn was far away, they found solace in each other's presence—a momentary peace before the inevitable storms ahead.
Outside their door, the world waited — relentless, harsh, and unforgiving. But inside, amid whispered fears and silent cries, two broken hearts beat as one, refusing to let go.

BETWEEN HOPE AND DESPAIR

The first light of dawn seeped through the cracked window panes, casting soft golden hues over the cluttered room. Ronak and Tarini sat side by side on the worn-out sofa, wrapped in a shared silence that was both comforting and heavy. Their exhaustion was not just physical — it was a fatigue born from fighting battles that seemed to have no end.

Tarini traced absent patterns on Ronak's palm, her eyes distant yet searching. "Do you ever wonder if we're just delaying the inevitable?" she whispered.

Ronak tightened his grip. "No. I believe in us. Even when it's hard to see the path."

Her lips quivered, a tear slipping down her cheek. "Sometimes, I wish I could escape this — all of it. The pressure, the fear... the feeling that I'm breaking apart."

He pulled her closer, resting his forehead against hers. "You're not alone. And you're stronger than you think."

But strength felt like a fragile illusion for Tarini. Each day was a tightrope walk between holding on and letting go.

That afternoon, a phone call shattered their fragile peace — news from Tarini's mother that deepened the rift between dreams and duty. Her family's insistence on an arranged marriage weighed heavily, threatening to tear apart the delicate bond Ronak and Tarini had fought so hard to protect.

The weeks that followed were a whirlwind of whispered plans, stolen moments, and promises made in shadows. They dreamed of running away, of building a life free from judgment and expectation. But every plan was shadowed by doubt and the heavy chains of reality.

One evening, beneath a sky heavy with storm clouds, Ronak held Tarini's face in his hands. "Whatever happens, I want you to remember — you are not alone. We are in this together."

Tears mixed with rain as Tarini nodded, their hearts beating together against the darkness.

CHAPTER THIRTEEN

SHADOWS OVER DREAMS

The storm arrived suddenly, dark and fierce, as if the sky itself was mirroring the turmoil in Ronak and Tarini's lives. Thunder growled low, and rain pounded relentlessly against the windows, drowning out the city's usual noise. Inside Tarini's small apartment, the atmosphere was thick with unspoken fears and creeping despair.

Ronak sat beside her on the worn couch, his hand clutching hers tightly. She was pale, her eyes rimmed red from sleepless nights and silent tears. Every tremble in her frame pulled at his heart like a sharp, unyielding ache.

"Tarini," he whispered gently, brushing a damp strand of hair from her face. "Please talk to me. Don't shut me out."

Her lips quivered as she looked away, voice barely above a whisper. "I'm scared, Ronak. So scared. Scared I won't be enough — for you, for myself. Scared that I'm losing everything I ever wanted... my dreams, my family, even you."

Ronak's chest tightened, pain cutting through him sharper than any blade. He wrapped his arms around her, holding her close as if sheer will could keep her from slipping away.

"We'll fight this. Together. No matter how hard it gets," he promised, voice raw with emotion.

But even as he spoke, he could see the weariness gnawing at her — a slow, insidious hunger draining her strength day by day.

Days blended into nights, and Tarini's fragile smile faded. She moved like a ghost through their shared world — present but distant, caught in a haze of exhaustion and despair.

One afternoon, Ronak returned home early, his heart pounding with a strange dread. He found her collapsed in the studio corner, paintbrush fallen from her trembling fingers onto the floor. Her breaths were shallow, face pale as chalk.

"Tarini!" he called out, panic surging through him as he rushed to her side. "What's wrong? Talk to me."

She tried to meet his eyes, but her voice was barely audible. "I... I don't know. I'm just so tired."

That moment shattered something deep inside Ronak — the terrifying realization that love and willpower might not be enough to save the girl he adored.

He sat beside her, heart heavy, fingers tracing hers as she lay exhausted.

"We'll get through this. I won't let you face it alone," he vowed quietly, though the weight of uncertainty pressed down on him like a stone.

Yet, amidst the growing shadows and uncertainty, their love remained — a fragile flame flickering against the encroaching darkness, a beacon of hope amid despair.

CHAPTER FOURTEEN

GHOSTS IN HER DIARY

The days blended into one another, a slow, painful march through shadows and uncertainty. The vibrant colors of life that once surrounded Tarini were fading, replaced by a muted palette of exhaustion and despair. Each morning, Ronak awoke with a sinking feeling, the sight of her fragile frame more haunting than the day before.

Her laughter, once a melody that filled every corner of their world, had grown rare — replaced by quiet sighs and distant gazes. The dreams they had woven together now felt like fragile threads stretched too thin, threatening to snap.

Ronak's world had shrunk to the size of their shared room, a small sanctuary where he tried to shield her from the harshness outside. He spent countless hours sitting beside her, holding her hand, tracing the contours of her face as if memorizing every detail in case she slipped away.

But the silence between them was deafening. Neither knew how to break it — how to voice the fears lurking deep within their hearts.

One evening, as the sun dipped low, casting long shadows across the balcony, Ronak gently took Tarini's hand. The cool evening breeze rustled the leaves below, carrying the distant hum of the city.

"Tarini," he whispered, voice thick with emotion, "if you could have anything in this world, what would it be?"

She looked up, her eyes shimmering with tears that refused to fall. "To be free. Free from the weight of expectations, from the fear that chains me. To live a life where I can simply be... myself."

Ronak swallowed hard, the lump in his throat threatening to choke him. "I wish I could give you that freedom. I wish I could carry all your pain for you."

Her faint smile was a fragile beacon in the gathering darkness. "Just having you here gives me strength. More than you know."

But beneath her words, Ronak saw the cracks — the growing exhaustion that no love alone could heal.

That night, as they lay entwined in each other's arms, the silence deepened. It was a silence heavy with unspoken fears, a quiet acknowledgment that love, no matter how fierce, might not be enough to hold back the darkness creeping closer with every passing day.

Ronak traced lazy circles on her back, willing himself to believe that their love could conquer all. But the weight of reality pressed down, cold and unyielding.

He pressed a kiss to her forehead, whispering, "We'll find a way. Together."

Yet, deep inside, a part of him trembled — terrified of the day when promises would not be enough.

CHAPTER FIFTEEN

FRACTURED PROMISES

The room was dimly lit by the flickering light of a lone candle, casting trembling shadows on the peeling walls. Outside, the relentless rain pattered against the window, a cold symphony that matched the heaviness inside Ronak's heart.

Tarini lay on the bed, her once radiant face now pale and drawn, a thin blanket barely keeping her warm. The vibrant spark that had always defined her spirit was dimming with each passing day, yet in her eyes was a flicker—a stubborn flame refusing to die out completely.

Ronak sat beside her, his hand enveloping hers gently, afraid that even the slightest pressure might cause her to slip away from him. His throat tightened as he struggled to find words strong enough to carry the weight of his emotions.

"I don't know how much longer I can be strong for both of us," he admitted, voice breaking. The vulnerability in his confession echoed loudly in the silence between them.

Tarini's fingers twitched, and she offered him a weak smile, her lips trembling. "You've been stronger than you realize. But you don't have to bear this burden alone."

He shook his head, desperation and helplessness bubbling to the surface. "I promised I'd be here for you. I meant it with every fiber of my being. But sometimes... sometimes I'm terrified that love alone won't be enough to save you."

Her eyes filled with tears—mirroring the anguish he felt inside—and she whispered, "Love is all I have left. It's the only thing that keeps me breathing, keeps me fighting. But sometimes, it feels so fragile, like a glass thread on the verge of snapping."

Ronak tightened his grip, leaning close so his words could reach her heart. "Then we'll fight with that fragile thread, Tarini. Together, we'll hold on, no matter how hard it gets."

Days turned into nights, and nights blurred into endless vigil. Ronak sought every possible help—doctors, specialists, alternative treatments—clinging to the slimmest chances. The cold, clinical words of the doctors cut through him like shards of ice. The prognosis was grim. The disease was merciless, relentless in its advance.

One gloomy afternoon, the rain drumming steadily against the window, Ronak sat by Tarini's bedside. Her breathing was shallow, each breath a small victory. Their hands remained entwined, a silent promise in the fading light.

"No matter what comes," Ronak vowed, voice raw but resolute, "I will never stop loving you. I will carry you in my heart, even if I lose you in this world."

A soft smile played on Tarini's lips, tears brimming in her eyes as she whispered back, "And I will carry your love with me, wherever I go. That's a promise no darkness can steal."

In that fragile moment between hope and despair, two souls made a vow—one that would echo beyond the pain, beyond the sorrow, binding them forever.
But fate, indifferent and cruel, was already writing its final chapter.

CHAPTER SIXTEEN

THE QUIET BEFORE GOODBYE

The city outside was wrapped in a shroud of mist and cold rain, a quiet melancholy that seemed to seep into every corner of Ronak's small apartment. Inside, the air was heavy with unspoken fears and fragile hopes, the stillness broken only by the faint, uneven breaths of Tarini lying on the bed.

She looked so small now—so fragile—a delicate flower wilting under the weight of a relentless winter. Her skin, once glowing with life and color, had turned pale, almost translucent. The vibrant spark in her eyes was flickering, battling against the darkness that threatened to swallow her whole.

Ronak sat beside her, his heart aching in a way words could never fully express. He held her hand gently, careful not to hurt the fragile thread of life that still connected them. His thumb traced slow circles on her palm, trying to convey all the love, all the strength he wished he could give her.

"Tarini," he whispered, voice barely audible in the quiet room, "can you hear me?"

Her eyelids fluttered open slowly, and she managed a faint smile, the kind that tried to mask the pain. "I hear you, Ronak. I always hear you."

He leaned closer, pressing his forehead against hers, seeking to transfer warmth through the simple touch. "I'm here. Always. And I'm not going anywhere."

For a long moment, they stayed like that, two souls entwined in a fragile bubble of love and time slipping away too quickly.

Then Tarini spoke again, her voice barely more than a breath, "Promise me something."

Ronak's heart clenched. "Anything."

"Promise me you'll live," she said, eyes searching his, "not just survive, but live. Really live — for yourself, for us, for the memories we made."

Tears welled up in Ronak's eyes as he nodded fiercely. "I promise. I will live. For you. I will carry you with me, always."

Her hand squeezed his weakly, tears streaming down her pale cheeks. "I love you, Ronak. Always."

"And I love you," he whispered, voice cracking, "more than words can say."

The rain outside began to fall softly, tapping against the windows like a gentle lullaby. They held onto each other, the world outside forgotten for a moment — two hearts beating as one against the approaching night.

But beneath the quiet, the shadow of goodbye loomed, a silent thief stealing away the moments they so desperately clung to.

Ronak stayed awake through the night, watching Tarini's chest rise and fall, memorizing every fragile breath. He whispered promises to her, pledges of eternal love and undying devotion, trying to hold back the

inevitable.
As dawn's first light crept through the curtains, Ronak knew their time was running out — that the quiet before goodbye was the cruelest silence of all.

CHAPTER SEVENTEEN

FRACTURED LIGHT

The morning was heavy with silence, broken only by the faint rustle of the rain still falling softly outside. The world seemed to slow to a crawl, as if nature itself paused to witness the fragile moments between life and the inevitable.

Inside the small room, the pale sunlight filtered through the thin curtains, casting delicate patterns on the cracked walls and the worn bed where Tarini lay, so still, so fragile. Her breath came in shallow whispers — shallow yet persistent, like a fading melody clinging to the last notes of a song.

Ronak sat beside her, his eyes never leaving her face. Every rise and fall of her chest sent a pang through his heart, a constant reminder of how precariously close they were to losing the most precious thing in his life. His fingers trembled as they clasped hers, afraid that the slightest movement might shatter the fragile connection they still shared.

His mind raced, flooded with memories — their first meeting, moments of laughter, stolen glances, promises whispered in the quiet of night. He saw her in every detail — the curve of her smile, the way her eyes lit up when she talked about her dreams, the warmth of her hand in his.

"Ronak," she breathed, her voice soft but steady, reaching through the haze to touch him. "You stayed with me."

"Always," he whispered, leaning down to press a gentle kiss to her forehead. "I promised I wouldn't leave."

Tears welled in her eyes, glistening like fragile stars. "I'm so sorry... for everything. For making you suffer."

He shook his head, his voice breaking. "You don't have to apologize. You're the strongest person I know."

Her fingers twitched weakly, seeking his. "Promise me something."

"Anything," he said, heart pounding.

"Promise me you'll forgive yourself," she said, voice barely above a whisper. "Don't carry the weight of my leaving."

Ronak's breath hitched. "How can I? How can I forgive myself if I lose you?"

Her eyes softened with love and sadness. "Because I don't want you to be broken. You have to live — really live. For both of us."

He pressed his lips to her hand, swallowing the lump in his throat. "I don't know how."

"You will," she said, smiling faintly. "Because love doesn't end here."

For a long while, they sat in silence, the world shrinking to just the two of them — bound by love, grief, and the unspoken understanding of what was coming.

Ronak's thoughts drifted back to brighter days, the laughter and joy that seemed so distant now. He remembered the first time Tarini had laughed so hard she cried, the way her eyes sparkled in the sunlight, the quiet moments they shared under the stars.

"Do you remember the jasmine tree?" she asked suddenly, her voice a fragile thread.

He nodded. "How could I forget? You said it was the most beautiful tree you'd ever seen."

She smiled weakly. "Because you were beneath it."

Ronak laughed softly, a bittersweet sound. "You made that day unforgettable."

Her eyes closed briefly as a cough shook her thin frame. He held her tighter, willing the pain to stop, willing the moment to last forever.

As the hours passed, her breaths grew more labored, but her spirit remained — fierce, beautiful, unwilling to fade quietly.

Ronak whispered stories, memories, promises — anything to keep her tethered to this world a little longer. And in those final moments, their love burned brighter than ever, a fragile flame that refused to be extinguished by the darkness closing in.

Then, with a final, trembling sigh, Tarini's hand slipped from his.

Ronak felt the world crack open, a silent scream trapped deep inside him. The room grew cold, empty, and the light seemed to dim.

He held onto the memory of her smile, the warmth of her touch, the echo of her love — a light to guide him through the darkest nights ahead.

CHAPTER EIGHTEEN

THE HOLLOW AFTERMATH

The room was suffocating in its silence. The emptiness left by Tarini's absence was not just physical, but a deep, hollow void that echoed through every corner of Ronak's being. The bed where she once lay, her soft breaths filling the space, now felt cold and lifeless — a cruel reminder of what he had lost.

Ronak sat on the edge, hands trembling as if expecting to feel her pulse beneath his fingers. But there was only stillness. The world outside continued on its indifferent course, but for Ronak, time had fractured, splintering into fragments too sharp and jagged to bear.

Days turned into nights without distinction. His once steady routine dissolved into a series of empty moments filled with aching loneliness. The sunlight that filtered through the window no longer warmed him; it only illuminated the shadows inside.

Family and friends came to offer condolences — their voices kind but distant, their words hollow against the tempest of grief raging inside him. "She's in a better place," they said. "Time will heal." But those words fell flat, unable to bridge the chasm tearing him apart.

Ronak barely ate. Food sat untouched on the table. Sleep was elusive, stolen by nightmares where Tarini's voice called to him, faint and fading. He woke in cold sweats, heart pounding, clutching at the sheets as if they could hold her close.

Every night, he replayed their last moments — the fragile promises, the soft confessions, the unbearable silence before the final goodbye. The memory was a knife twisting endlessly in his chest.

Yet, somewhere deep in the wreckage of his soul, a faint glimmer flickered. It was the memory of her last words, whispered with such fragile strength: "Live, Ronak. Really live."

That promise became a lifeline. A reason to breathe.

One morning, with hands shaky and eyes swollen from sleepless nights, Ronak left the confines of his apartment. He walked aimlessly, drawn toward the jasmine tree where they had first met — that sacred place where laughter had once bloomed, untouched by sorrow.

Sitting beneath the familiar branches, he let the tears fall freely, the soft fragrance of jasmine wrapping around him like a bittersweet embrace. He spoke aloud to the quiet air, words he wished she could hear.

"I don't know how to live without you," he admitted, voice breaking. "But I'll try. For you. For us."

The rustling leaves seemed to answer, a gentle whisper in the breeze, and for a moment, he felt her presence — like a fragile thread connecting his broken heart to a love that would never truly die.

Days passed, and Ronak forced himself to take small steps. He cleaned the apartment, put away her things carefully, preserving her memory without letting it imprison him. He visited places they had dreamed of exploring, carrying her in his heart as he tried to rediscover the world through eyes tinged with grief and hope.

His pain remained, a constant ache beneath the surface, but slowly, it began to soften, edged by resilience born from love and loss.

One evening, standing beneath the stars they once wished upon, Ronak whispered into the night, "I promise I'll live — for you, Tarini. Your love will be my light."

And in that moment, amidst the vast darkness, he felt a fragile peace — the beginning of healing, born from the depths of heartbreak.

CHAPTER NINETEEN

A Flicker in the Darkness

The days stretched endlessly after Tarini's departure, each one heavier than the last, yet slowly, imperceptibly, a change began to stir within Ronak — like the first faint light before dawn, fragile but undeniable.

In the early mornings, he would sit beneath the jasmine tree where they had first met, letting the soft fragrance wash over him like a bittersweet memory. The world around him was still shadowed by grief, but the tree — with its delicate white blossoms trembling in the breeze — seemed to offer a quiet promise: life goes on, even after loss.

Ronak's heart still ached fiercely, but the sharp edges of despair softened as he allowed himself to remember the joy as well as the sorrow. He whispered to the empty air, telling Tarini stories about the days they had dreamed of, the plans they had made — as if speaking aloud might bring her closer, even if only for a moment.

Some nights, tears would flow freely, a cleansing river washing over his soul. Other nights, he found himself smiling faintly, recalling the warmth of her smile, the sound of her laughter, the way her eyes sparkled when she spoke of hope and dreams.

Slowly, he began to open his heart to others. Friends who had stood quietly by his side reached out with gentle words and patient understanding. They did not rush him to heal, nor push him to forget. Instead, they offered their presence — a quiet comfort in the storm.

One afternoon, wandering through a bustling market, Ronak's eyes fell upon a small, weathered bookstall. Amidst stacks of old novels and forgotten journals, a simple notebook with a worn leather cover caught his attention. There was no grand title, just a few faint floral embossments — yet something about it pulled at him. He bought the notebook without hesitation, feeling as if it held a purpose meant just for him.

That night, under the dim glow of a lamp, Ronak opened the notebook and began to write. At first, it was just fragmented thoughts and memories — a sketch of Tarini's laughter, the softness of her touch, the ache of her absence. But as the pages filled, writing became his sanctuary — a place where grief transformed into something tangible, where love could live on in words.

Through his writing, Ronak found a way to channel his pain, to give shape to the swirling emotions within him. He wrote about their dreams, their first meeting, the promises they had made. Each word was a step forward, a thread woven into the tapestry of healing.

Life outside his grief began to seep back into his world. He noticed the blush of dawn breaking over the rooftops, the soft murmur of the river nearby, the innocent laughter of children playing in the street. These small moments, once unnoticed, now shimmered with fragile beauty.

Ronak took tentative steps toward rebuilding a life —
one that honored Tarini's memory without being
consumed by it. He visited places they had talked about
exploring, walked through gardens they had dreamed of
wandering, carried her spirit with him like a gentle flame
lighting his way.

One evening, as the sky blazed with the colors of sunset
— fiery oranges melting into soft pinks — Ronak stood
beneath the jasmine tree. The blossoms fluttered gently in
the breeze, a silent witness to love, loss, and the fragile
hope that remained.

He whispered, voice thick with emotion, "I'm trying,
Tarini. For you. For us."

Though the ache in his chest lingered, he felt a flicker
of light — a delicate flame of hope, small but steady,
illuminating the path ahead.

And in that moment, amidst the quiet beauty of dusk,
Ronak understood that healing was not forgetting, but
learning to carry love through the darkest nights.

CHAPTER TWENTY

STEPS TOWARD TOMORROW

The jasmine tree, once a silent witness to young love and tender promises, had become a sacred refuge for Ronak. Each time he sat beneath its blossoming branches, the delicate white petals drifting in the breeze felt like fragments of Tarini's spirit — gentle reminders that though she was gone, her presence lingered in the world around him.

His life, however, was far from simple. The days after Tarini's passing had stretched into a fog of grief and numbness, but now, months later, he found himself at the cusp of awakening — though the path was steep and jagged, littered with memories that both comforted and shattered him anew.

Returning to work was a trial he hadn't anticipated. The office walls, once neutral and mundane, now seemed charged with echoes of the past — the faint scent of her favorite jasmine tea, the way her laughter might have filled the space, the way he had imagined sharing future dreams over late-night conversations. His colleagues treated him with gentle kindness, some offering quiet nods of understanding, others trying awkwardly to break through the barrier of his sorrow.

Days were filled with a careful balance — showing up even when his heart threatened to collapse, answering emails with a distracted mind, trying to focus but often drifting into memories. At night, he would collapse into his bed, exhausted not just from work but from the emotional weight he carried.

His friends became his lifeline. They knew words alone could never mend his broken heart, but their presence — steady and patient — was a balm he didn't realize he desperately needed. They dragged him out of his solitude with hesitant invitations to dinners, movies, and quiet walks through familiar streets. Sometimes he resisted; other times, he found himself smiling, the first genuine smiles in weeks.

At home, the apartment was a shrine to their shared past. Tarini's belongings remained carefully preserved — her favorite scarf folded gently on the dresser, the small jar of jasmine perfume sitting on a shelf where the light caught it just so, the scattered pages of a notebook filled with their dreams. Ronak was torn between the desire to hold onto every token and the painful need to begin letting go.

One evening, the loneliness pressed in on him so fiercely that he opened the notebook and began to write — words flowing slowly at first, then with increasing urgency. He wrote of Tarini's laughter, the sparkle in her eyes, the dreams they had once spun together like fragile webs of hope. He wrote of the pain, the emptiness, the desperate longing to turn back time. But beneath it all, there was a growing resolve — a promise that her love would not be forgotten.

With each word, Ronak felt a small piece of his heart begin to stitch itself back together.

Outside, life moved in bursts of color and sound. Ronak noticed the blush of dawn as it crept over the city skyline, the soft murmur of the river nearby, the innocent laughter of children playing in the street. These small moments — once invisible or taken for granted — now shimmered with a fragile beauty that he was learning to cherish.

He started to explore the world again, hesitantly at first. He visited the hilltop they had once dreamed of climbing, feeling the wind against his face and imagining Tarini beside him. He walked along the riverbank at dusk, tracing the path of their whispered conversations beneath the stars. He even spoke to strangers — brief exchanges that reminded him he was still part of a living, breathing world.

One day, while walking through a crowded marketplace, a little girl darted past him chasing a bright yellow kite. Her laughter rang out, pure and joyful — a sound that stirred something deep inside Ronak. He smiled through his tears, recognizing in her the same light that had once shone so brightly in Tarini's eyes.

That evening, under the jasmine tree, as twilight painted the sky in hues of gold and violet, Ronak closed his eyes and whispered a vow to the night:

"I will live, Tarini. For you, for us. I will carry your light with me — even when the darkness threatens to swallow me whole."

The ache in his chest was still there, a persistent shadow, but it was no longer all-consuming. It had softened, becoming a quiet companion — a reminder of love that endured beyond death.

Ronak understood now that healing was not a straight path, nor a sudden transformation. It was a series of small steps — moments of courage, glimpses of hope, and the willingness to keep moving forward even when the way was unclear.

And so, beneath the gentle sway of jasmine branches and the vastness of the starry sky, Ronak took a deep breath and stepped toward tomorrow — carrying Tarini's memory as both a burden and a blessing.

CHAPTER TWENTY-ONE

The Quiet Awakening

The jasmine tree had become more than just a place for Ronak — it was a sacred space where the past and present met, where grief was held gently between memories and new beginnings. Its delicate white blossoms, fragrant in the soft breeze, seemed to carry whispers of Tarini's laughter, her hopes, her dreams. Every time Ronak sat beneath its branches, he felt both her absence and her presence — a paradox that both comforted and tore at his heart.

The months after her death had been an endless battle against the heavy fog of despair. Yet now, slowly but surely, something within Ronak began to shift. It was subtle at first, almost imperceptible: a moment's smile at a memory, a softening in the tightness around his chest, a breath that didn't catch with sorrow. These were small awakenings, fragile as the jasmine petals falling softly around him, but they carried the weight of survival.

Ronak's mornings often began with long walks to the tree. Sometimes he brought his notebook, pouring out words that tasted of loss and love, grief and hope. Other times, he simply sat, eyes closed, breathing in the scent of jasmine and the city around him. The city buzzed with life, a relentless tide of sound and motion, but here beneath the tree, time slowed, allowing him space to breathe.

Work was no longer the enemy. It had once seemed a hollow routine, a reminder of the future that would never be, but now it was a lifeline. Each email answered, each meeting attended was a small victory — proof that he could still function, still face the world. His colleagues' support was quiet and unassuming, a network of kindness that steadied him without overwhelming.

Friends, too, remained anchors. They understood that healing was not a race, that grief could not be hurried or forced aside. Their invitations to dinners, movies, and walks were gentle reminders that life persisted — and that he was not alone. Often, these outings ended in comfortable silences or half-spoken words, the kind that come only from deep trust.

Yet the nights were the hardest. When the city quieted and the walls closed in, Ronak wrestled with an emptiness that threatened to swallow him whole. Memories surged like waves — the warmth of Tarini's hand in his, the sparkle in her eyes when she laughed, the dreams they'd painted together in the glow of twilight. He learned to sit with these moments, letting the tears fall freely, not shying away from the pain but embracing it as part of the journey.

One afternoon, as he sifted through letters and papers Tarini had left behind, a folded envelope slipped out from between the pages of a book. Inside was an invitation to a charity event supporting cancer research — a cause Tarini had devoted herself to with fierce passion. The invitation was both a sting and a beacon, a reminder of all they had lost and the fight she had carried until the end.

After days of hesitation, Ronak decided to attend. The event was held in a grand hall filled with people whose eyes held stories of hope and heartbreak. As he moved through the crowd, he felt an unexpected connection — a silent understanding shared among strangers who had faced similar losses. Conversations sparked, gentle smiles were exchanged, and for the first time in months, Ronak laughed — a laugh that came unbidden, raw and real.

That night, walking home beneath a sky crowded with stars, Ronak felt the weight of his grief lighten, if only a little. The jasmine tree loomed ahead, its blossoms glowing softly in the moonlight. He stopped beneath its branches and whispered to the night, "I will live, Tarini. For you, for us. And for the chance to find light, even in the deepest darkness."

The ache in his heart remained, a quiet companion that would never fully leave. But alongside it, a fragile hope was beginning to bloom — a promise that life, with all its pain and beauty, could still be embraced.

And so, beneath the gentle sway of jasmine petals and the vastness of the night sky, Ronak took a breath — deep and steady — and stepped forward into the uncertain light of tomorrow.

CHAPTER TWENTY-TWO

THE FRAGILE BLOOM

The city around Ronak never paused. It flowed endlessly, a torrent of sound, light, and movement, indifferent to the sorrow of one young man beneath its sprawling skyline. And yet, within this vast, unyielding tide, Ronak began to sense a subtle shift — a quiet pulse that whispered of possibility, even amid the shadows.

Each morning, long before dawn, he would sit by his bedroom window and watch the world awake. The city lights dimmed slowly, replaced by the soft glow of the rising sun. The sky deepened from inky black to hues of lavender and gold. It was a daily miracle, a reminder that despite the weight of grief pressing on his chest, time itself continued to move forward, carrying with it the chance for healing.

Sometimes, as the cool morning air brushed his face, Ronak imagined Tarini there beside him. He pictured her hair catching the first light, her eyes sparkling with quiet hope, her hand slipping gently into his. These moments were both balm and burden — a bittersweet ache of presence in absence.

Work remained a constant, a rhythm he clung to. But between the hours spent in meetings and emails, the real battles raged in the quiet spaces — the long nights when memories flooded back unbidden, the moments of loneliness that wrapped around him like a heavy cloak. Yet amidst this sorrow, he began to notice flickers of light: a smile shared with a stranger on a crowded street, the distant sound of children's laughter spilling through open windows, the scent of jasmine carried on the breeze.

One afternoon, drawn by impulse and the need for something new, Ronak wandered into a small, unassuming art gallery tucked away in a side street he rarely visited. Inside, the walls were alive with color and emotion — paintings depicting raw human experience, from heartbreak to hope, from despair to resilience.

He stood long before one painting in particular — a solitary tree, battered by a storm, yet standing tall with roots dug deep into the earth and branches reaching toward a turbulent sky. The image resonated deeply, mirroring the turmoil within his own heart.

A gentle voice broke his reverie. An elderly woman, the gallery's curator, approached and spoke softly about the artist, a woman who had transformed her own grief into powerful works of art. Their conversation became a quiet sharing of loss and survival, a tender reminder that pain, when faced and expressed, could give rise to unexpected beauty.

That evening, walking home beneath a sky painted in the soft pastels of sunset, Ronak felt an unfamiliar sensation stirring within — a fragile glimmer of hope, delicate and tentative but undeniable.

Returning to the jasmine tree, he knelt and laid his hand on its bark, grounding himself in the present moment. "Tarini," he whispered, voice trembling, "I'm still here. I'm still trying to live."

Days passed, and slowly, imperceptibly, Ronak began to open himself more — to friends who stood patiently by, to new experiences that challenged his fear of moving forward, to the possibility that joy could coexist with sorrow.

He allowed himself laughter more often, the kind that came from genuine moments rather than forced smiles. He dreamed again, carefully at first, of futures where pain was not erased but held gently alongside hope.

Still, Tarini's memory remained a constant presence — a thread woven through every breath, every heartbeat. In the quiet hours of the night, he would speak to her softly, sharing fears and triumphs alike, seeking comfort in the imagined echo of her voice.

Though the journey of healing was far from complete, Ronak felt the first stirrings of renewal within his soul. Like the jasmine blossoms that bloomed fragile and bright beneath the moonlight, his heart began to bloom anew — tentative, delicate, but alive.

And in that fragile bloom lay the promise that even the deepest wounds could, in time, give rise to new life.

CHAPTER TWENTY-THREE

ECHOES IN THE SILENCE

The days that followed settled like a slow, steady rhythm, a fragile pulse beneath the surface of Ronak's life. Time no longer blurred into an endless stretch of pain but began to mark itself in moments — moments of quiet reflection, unexpected smiles, and gentle reminders of Tarini's enduring presence.

The jasmine tree outside his window stood witness to his transformation. Its delicate blossoms, soft and white, floated down like silent blessings, landing gently on the earth. Sometimes, when the breeze caught them just right, it felt as if the tree whispered to him — reminders of love lost but never forgotten.

One morning, just as the city was waking, Ronak's phone rang. It was Meera, a friend of Tarini's who Ronak had only met briefly once before. Her voice was soft but steady, carrying a warmth that reached across the distance and into the hollow spaces of his heart.

"Ronak," she began, "I have something of Tarini's I think you should see. It's... well, it's a collection of her writings — poems and reflections she never shared with many. She wanted you to have them."

Curious and cautious, Ronak agreed to meet Meera that afternoon in a quiet café tucked away from the noise of the city. When she handed him the manuscript, Ronak felt the weight of it — fragile, intimate, and raw, like a piece of Tarini's soul pressed onto the pages.

Back in his apartment, he opened the book with trembling hands. Tarini's handwriting was neat but alive, each word infused with the depth of her feelings and thoughts. The poems spoke of love's beauty and pain, of fleeting moments and eternal memories, of hope clinging to the edge of despair.

As Ronak read, he was transported back to the moments they had shared — the quiet mornings over chai, the stolen glances in crowded rooms, the laughter and dreams whispered beneath the stars. Each poem was a thread connecting him to her, a lifeline woven from sorrow and love.

That evening, he sat beneath the jasmine tree, the book resting on his knees. The sky was painted in soft purples and blues, the first stars beginning to twinkle. He read aloud, his voice mingling with the gentle rustle of leaves and the distant hum of the city.

Tears slid down his cheeks, but they were no longer just tears of heartbreak. They carried a complex mix of grief and gratitude, loss and hope. He realized that Tarini's love was not gone — it had transformed into something eternal, a light within him that no darkness could extinguish.

The days that followed were filled with small, precious moments. Ronak began to notice beauty again — the way sunlight filtered through the curtains in the morning, the sound of rain tapping rhythmically on the rooftop, the kindness of friends who patiently stood by him without pressure or judgment.

One afternoon, while wandering through a bustling market, he stopped as the notes of a street flute caught his attention. The melody was haunting and tender, weaving sorrow and hope into a single breath. Ronak closed his eyes, letting the music wash over him, reminding him that even in the depths of grief, life held fragments of beauty.

Later that night, back in the quiet solitude of his apartment, Ronak placed Tarini's book on the shelf beside a small vase of jasmine blossoms. He lit a candle, its soft glow flickering against the shadows.

Whispering into the stillness, he made a promise. "I will carry you with me, Tarini. Your light will guide me when the darkness feels too heavy."

Though the road ahead remained uncertain, and the ache of loss lingered like a quiet echo, Ronak felt a fragile peace blooming within him. A hope that, step by step, moment by moment, he could learn to live again — carrying Tarini's memory not as a weight, but as a gentle wind beneath his wings.

CHAPTER TWENTY-FOUR

THE SHADOWS AND THE LIGHT

The city was alive around Ronak — a relentless, humming presence that seemed indifferent to his quiet grief. Traffic lights blinked, voices rose and fell, vendors called out to passing crowds, and somewhere nearby, a train rumbled by. Yet inside Ronak, there was a silence so vast it felt as if it stretched into infinity, a silence shaped by loss and the weight of absence.

The jasmine tree outside his window had become more than just a tree; it was a living symbol of everything Tarini had meant to him. Its branches curved protectively, the delicate white flowers falling like tears on the ground below. Often, Ronak would sit beneath it, tracing patterns in the fallen petals, letting the familiar scent wrap around him like a fragile comfort.

Work pressed on him with its usual demands, but lately it felt heavier, harder to bear. His mind wandered, memories seeping into his thoughts at unexpected moments — Tarini's laughter echoing in a quiet room, the softness of her hand in his, the dreams they had spun together like fragile webs. Sometimes the pain was so sharp it caught his breath and left him gasping. Other times, it was a dull ache, a companion in the lonely nights.

One evening, Ronak received a message from Meera. She invited him to a small gathering — a group of people brought together by shared loss and the journey toward healing. The invitation stirred a complex mix of emotions — a longing for connection and a fear of opening old wounds.

After a restless night, Ronak decided to go. The meeting was held in a modest room softly lit by warm lamps, walls lined with books and cushions arranged in a circle. People came and went, each carrying their own stories etched in pain and hope.

As each person spoke, Ronak felt the weight of grief take shape in new ways — stories of love lost too soon, of regrets that lingered, and of the slow, fragile steps toward acceptance. When his turn came, his voice was unsteady. He spoke of Tarini — her boundless kindness, the light in her eyes, the dreams that death had tried to steal but couldn't quite touch.

He shared his own journey — the despair, the moments of numbness, the tiny sparks of hope that began to kindle again. The room listened without judgment, their silent empathy offering a rare and precious comfort.

Afterwards, stepping into the cool night air, Ronak felt a subtle shift. Though the ache remained, he sensed that grief was no longer a solitary prison. It was a path shared by many, a burden lightened by the weight of compassion.

A few days later, while tidying his apartment, Ronak discovered an old box Tarini had left behind. Inside were letters, photographs, pressed flowers, and small keepsakes — fragments of a life that had touched his so deeply.

He unfolded a letter addressed to him in Tarini's flowing handwriting. The words were a lifeline:
"My dearest Ronak,
If you are reading this, it means I am no longer by your side. But know this — my love for you transcends even death. Live bravely, love deeply, and find joy in the little things. I will be with you, always."
Tears blurred his vision as he clutched the letter close to his heart. In that moment, he felt both the sting of loss and the warmth of enduring love. "I will try, Tarini," he whispered into the stillness. "I promise."
That night, beneath the jasmine tree, Ronak allowed himself a rare moment of peace. The stars above twinkled softly, the scent of jasmine filling the cool air. He dreamed — not of the past, but of a future shaped by memory and love, pain and hope intertwined.
Though shadows lingered, so did the light — a fragile flame that flickered steadily, promising new beginnings even in the deepest darkness.

CHAPTER TWENTY-FIVE

THE LAST PROMISE

The morning dawned soft and golden, the city slowly stretching awake beneath a sky brushed with pale hues of rose and lavender. Outside Ronak's window, the jasmine tree stood tall and quiet, its branches heavy with blossoms that drifted down like gentle snowflakes, carrying the faintest scent of spring. The fragrance was subtle yet persistent — a delicate reminder of Tarini, lingering in the spaces she once filled with laughter and light.

Ronak stood beneath that tree, his palms pressed lightly against its rough bark, eyes closed as he breathed in the scent. The jasmine had become a symbol — a living monument to the love that had once bloomed fiercely between them, and to the grief that had almost consumed him after her passing. But now, beneath the fragile petals, he felt something new stirring: the slow, steady pulse of healing.

In his hand, he held Tarini's final letter, worn and creased from years of careful reading. It was a letter he had read countless times, but today, its words seemed to speak to him with a clarity and strength he hadn't known before.

"My dearest Ronak,
If you are reading this, it means I am no longer by your side.
But know this — my love for you transcends even death. Live
bravely, love deeply, and find joy in the little things. I will be
with you, always."

He folded the letter gently, holding it close to his chest as a tear slipped down his cheek. The pain of loss was still there — a quiet ache beneath the surface — but it no longer felt like a crushing weight. Instead, it was a thread connecting him to Tarini's memory, a bond that death could never sever.

Today was the day of the memorial gathering Meera had organized, a chance to celebrate Tarini's life and the indelible mark she had left on those who knew her. For weeks, Ronak had wrestled with the decision to attend. Part of him feared that the memories would flood back too fiercely, that the grief would overwhelm the fragile peace he'd fought so hard to find.

But now, as he looked up at the brightening sky and felt the gentle sway of jasmine petals in the breeze, he knew that this was not a farewell. It was a beginning — a step toward embracing the love and loss that shaped him, and a promise to carry Tarini's light forward.

The garden where the memorial was held was a quiet haven tucked away from the city's noise — a place where sunlight filtered softly through the leaves, casting dappled shadows on the faces gathered beneath the trees. Friends, family, and even strangers who had come to know Tarini through Meera's stories had gathered, each holding a piece of her in their hearts.

Voices rose and fell like a delicate symphony of remembrance. People shared stories — of Tarini's kindness that had brightened lonely days, her fierce courage in the face of illness, the way she had reached out to others with open hands and an open heart. Each memory was a spark, illuminating the darkness with warmth and love.

Ronak listened quietly, tears pricking at the corners of his eyes as he heard about moments he hadn't known — small acts of kindness, secret dreams, and the ways Tarini had touched lives beyond his own.

When it was his turn, Ronak stepped forward slowly, heart pounding but steady. He scanned the faces before him — eyes filled with compassion, understanding, and shared grief. Taking a deep breath, he began.

"I stand here today not only in sorrow but in gratitude," he said, his voice steady though emotions churned beneath the surface. "For Tarini — for every smile, every moment, every dream we shared. She taught me what it means to love without conditions, to face life's challenges with courage, and to find light even in the darkest places."

He paused, swallowing the lump in his throat as memories of her flooded his mind — the way her eyes sparkled when she laughed, the softness of her touch, the quiet strength that had carried them both through hard times.

"Though she is no longer with us," he continued, "her love lives on. It is a flame that burns brightly inside me — a light I promise to carry, no matter how dark the path may seem."

The crowd was silent, the weight of his words settling like a gentle embrace.

"I promise you all, and most of all, I promise her," Ronak said, voice growing stronger, "that I will live for both of us. I will honor her memory by living fully — with kindness, bravery, and love."

As he stepped back, the garden seemed to hold its breath. Then, softly, the crowd began to clap — a quiet, heartfelt applause that filled the space with warmth and connection.

Later, after the memorial, Ronak returned to the jasmine tree. The sun hung low, casting long shadows and painting the sky in hues of amber and gold. The petals swirled gently around him, a silent shower of blessings falling with the breeze.

He knelt down, brushing the blossoms aside and planting a small sapling nearby — a promise of growth, renewal, and the cycle of life.

Sitting back against the tree's sturdy trunk, Ronak closed his eyes and whispered into the quiet twilight, "Thank you, Tarini. For every moment we shared, every dream we dreamed. I will carry you with me, always."

The night deepened, stars emerging like distant beacons. In that stillness, Ronak felt a profound peace — not the absence of pain, but a presence of love that transcended loss.

His journey was far from over. There would be days of loneliness, moments of doubt, and times when the past threatened to swallow him whole. But now, he knew he was not alone. Tarini's love was a light within him, a fragile flame that would guide his steps into whatever future awaited.

Rising slowly, Ronak took a deep breath and looked toward the horizon, where the first stars twinkled in the darkening sky. With a heart heavy yet hopeful, he stepped forward — carrying Tarini's memory like a sacred promise, lighting the way through the shadows.

CHAPTER TWENTY-SIX

THE VOID

The garden was empty now.

The last of the guests had gone home. The chairs were folded, the flowers gathered into silent bundles. Even the wind that had whispered through the trees during the memorial seemed to have stilled, as if in mourning itself.

Ronak stood alone under the jasmine tree, the shadows of dusk stretching long across the earth. In one hand, he still held the folded letter Tarini had written to him — the edges worn soft, the ink smudged slightly by tears and time. The other hand rested on the bark of the tree, grounding him.

But inside?

Inside, there was only a vast silence. A vacuum. A screaming kind of stillness that didn't let him breathe. The pain had dulled over the months — the raw, tearing grief replaced by something quieter but heavier. Something that sat on his chest every morning and followed him into every room. There were no more breakdowns in public. No more collapsing onto the floor, fists clenched in disbelief. He had moved past those storms.

But now there was *this*.

The emptiness.

He turned away from the garden and walked toward his car, parked just outside the old gate. The drive home was slow. Familiar streets blurred past, lit with flickering lamps and neon signs he didn't read anymore. They were meaningless. The world hadn't stopped after Tarini's death. It never did. The world kept moving, without permission, without apology.

That night, back in his flat, Ronak didn't turn on the lights. He dropped his keys onto the kitchen counter and walked into the living room, collapsing onto the sofa like a puppet with its strings cut.

The silence pressed against his ears.

There were reminders of her everywhere. The little clay bird she once painted sat on the window sill. A book she had left half-read still lay beside the bed. Her handwriting on a sticky note still clung to the mirror — *"Don't forget your smile, it looks good on you."*

He hadn't smiled in days.

He hadn't spoken to anyone properly in weeks. Sometimes he wondered what people meant when they said "time heals." Because time, as he knew it now, didn't bring peace. It just brought distance. A growing stretch between the last moment he held her hand and the unbearable now. He was terrified that one day, even her voice in his memory would fade — the curve of her laugh, the tilt of her head when she teased him, the rhythm of her breathing when she fell asleep in his arms.

He didn't want healing if it meant forgetting.

Ronak got up and walked to the small drawer beneath his writing desk. He reached into the very back, where the velvet-covered box lay hidden. Slowly, with shaking fingers, he opened it.

Inside were Tarini's letters. Twenty of them.

She had written them during her last months — one for each chapter of his life she had hoped to witness. Some were sealed. Some had small doodles on the envelopes — stars, coffee mugs, mountains. All of them were numbered.

He had read only the first one.

He picked up the second.

Letter 2: "For when the world feels too quiet"

My love,

If you're holding this, you're probably drowning in the silence. I know that silence. It's sharp. It cuts deeper than noise ever could. But please don't run from it. Let it teach you something.

I used to fear silence too — until I met you. You filled my quiet places with light. And now, even if I can't be there, I want you to find that light again.

Turn on the music. The one I used to dance to when you were pretending not to look. Make tea the way I liked it — too sweet. Read my favorite poem out loud.

Let the silence know that it doesn't win.

Yours,

Tarini

Ronak held the letter to his chest and closed his eyes.

Then, slowly, he rose.

He walked to the kitchen and boiled water, adding too much sugar to the tea just like she liked. He put on her favorite playlist. He listened to that one song — the one she twirled to in the kitchen, barefoot, her scarf flying like a comet behind her.

The silence didn't go away.

But for a moment, it bent.

It made space.

That night, for the first time in months, Ronak picked up his pen and wrote in his journal. Not a poem, not a story. Just a sentence:

"She taught me that grief is love with nowhere to go — but maybe now, I can start giving it a direction."

And just like that, the void cracked open.

Just a little.

But enough to let in a breath of air.

CHAPTER TWENTY-SEVEN

LETTERS SHE LEFT

Morning bled into Ronak's apartment like a pale ghost — soft, hesitant, and almost unwilling. The city had already awakened; the honking of autos, temple bells, and murmured prayers drifted in through the half-open window. But inside Ronak's home, time moved differently. Slower. Heavier.

He hadn't slept. Not properly. After reading Tarini's second letter the previous night, he'd spent hours just sitting on the edge of the bed, the letter clutched in his hand like a lifeline. He hadn't cried. Not because the pain had vanished — it hadn't. But because sometimes, pain was too deep for tears.

He placed the letter gently beside the first one and reached into the velvet box again. The others were still there, untouched, waiting. Twenty letters in total — and he didn't even know when she had written them. She must have known she wouldn't make it. That realization twisted something inside him.

Why hadn't she told him?

Or maybe... she *had* told him — in the only way she knew how. With her eyes. Her long silences. Her sudden urge to capture moments. The endless photographs, the impulsive trips, the way she clung to him a little tighter after each goodbye.

He hadn't seen it then. He had been too in love, too wrapped in the illusion that they had more time.

Ronak lifted another envelope.

This one had a small drawing of a pen and paper, and a little heart above it. On the back, in her slanted, hurried handwriting were the words: *"Open this when you're scared to write."*

He smiled bitterly. How well she had known him.

He hesitated for a moment before opening it.

Letter 3: "When the words feel heavy"

Dearest Ronak,

If you're reading this, I know your hands are probably shaking, and your heart feels too full to fit inside your chest. Writing has always been your soul's language — but I also know how cruel it can feel when your soul is hurting.

I hope you haven't given up on your stories.

You always said your characters were pieces of you. So don't abandon them now. They're waiting — not just for you to finish their tales, but to help you process *ours*.

I don't want to be the chapter that ends your book.

Make me the reason you write harder. Write about pain, about loss, about the way we laughed until we couldn't breathe. Write about love — the messy, beautiful, terrifying kind we had.

If nothing else, write to me.

I'll always be listening.

Yours — forever and some more,

Tarini

Ronak folded the letter with trembling hands. His throat burned.

He sat at the old wooden desk by the window — the same desk where Tarini once leaned over to correct his spelling in a poem and spilled chai all over his rough draft. The stain was still there. He hadn't sanded it away. He never could.

Outside, the jasmine tree moved gently in the breeze. It was in bloom again. Just like the day she left.

He pulled open his notebook. The pages had yellowed. The pen felt awkward between his fingers, like a stranger. He hadn't written a single word since Tarini's death — not even a grocery list. It was as if the ink had dried up inside him the moment her heartbeat stopped.

But now... now he had something.

A voice again.

Her voice.

He started with her name.

Tarini.

Then he wrote the words she had once whispered into his neck during a storm: *"If you ever lose me, just remember — I chose you, always. Even in the end."*

And suddenly, the words came like rain. Gentle at first. Then faster. And heavier. They poured out of him — not as poetry, but as truth. Not pretty, not polished — but *real*.

His journal filled with thoughts, fragments of conversations they never got to finish, memories wrapped in pain and laughter.

Hours passed.

Ronak didn't even notice when the sun shifted and the light grew warmer. He didn't answer his phone. He didn't check his messages. For the first time in months, he wasn't looking at the past through a window — he was *inside it*, living it again, grieving it honestly.

And it wasn't just grief.

It was love.

Still there. Still warm. Still alive.

That evening, he sat by the jasmine tree with the three letters in his lap. He didn't open more. Not yet. Each letter was a sacred moment, a conversation stolen from time.

Instead, he lit a candle — one of the ones Tarini had bought from the old shop in Pondicherry. Lavender. Her favorite. The flame danced as the wind teased it, but it didn't go out.

Neither did he.

He looked up at the sky. The stars were slowly appearing, one by one — just like she had once told him they would.

"Even when they're gone, their light keeps traveling."

Ronak smiled through the ache.

"Yes, Tarini," he whispered. "Your light is still reaching me."

And he knew then — she hadn't left him completely.

She never would.

As long as the letters remained.

As long as her words lived in him.

She would never truly be gone.

CHAPTER TWENTY-EIGHT

THE BROKEN PEN

The following days unfolded like an old film reel — grainy, slow, flickering in sepia tones.

Ronak drifted through them, half-awake and half-asleep, pulled between the heaviness of grief and the fragile thread of memory that kept Tarini close. Writing had helped — for a night. But healing wasn't linear. It was a spiral, pulling him in and spitting him out, sometimes in the same hour.

This morning, the world felt muted again.

No letters today, he decided. He wasn't ready. Last night's dreams had been too cruel — vivid flashes of Tarini laughing, reaching for his hand, disappearing in a blur of light just as he touched her fingers. He had woken up with a soaked pillow, his chest tight, his lungs aching as if he'd been screaming underwater.

He sat at his desk again anyway.

The pen in his hand was her favorite — a slim, matte blue one with a golden nib. She used to steal it from him and doodle on napkins. "This pen makes words prettier," she'd say, always smiling, always making everything lighter.

He held it like he was holding her hand.

His fingers moved slowly, sketching out her name again on the page.

Tarini.

And then it happened — a sudden snap, sharp and loud in the silent room.

The pen broke.

The nib bent. The barrel cracked. A line of ink spilled across the page, a violent black slash over her name. It spread like blood.

Ronak froze.

His heart jumped.

He stared at the ruined page, the broken pen lying like a body in his hand. And something inside him crumbled. All at once. Without warning.

He pushed the chair back and fell to his knees on the cold floor, the pen still clenched tightly in his palm.

"No," he whispered. "No, no, no—"

It wasn't about the pen.

It was about everything.

The months he hadn't cried. The days he'd faked being strong. The mornings he woke up hoping, just for a second, that it was all a dream. The smiles he had forced at her memorial. The endless, aching silence that followed.

The broken pen was just the final blow — the last thread that held together his pretend normal.

And now, there was nothing left.

He wept.

Not quietly. Not gracefully. But the way only someone who had truly loved — and truly lost — could cry. His chest heaved. His fists pounded the floor. He sobbed her name again and again until it broke inside his mouth.

"Tarini..."

He wasn't sure how long he lay there.

When he finally sat up, the world looked blurred, smeared by grief and exhaustion. His breath came in sharp, jagged waves. His shirt was damp. His eyes burned. And yet, beneath all the mess of it — there was something else.
Relief.
He had finally *let it out.*
He reached up and pulled down the box of Tarini's belongings from the top shelf of his cupboard — something he hadn't dared to open since the hospital. Inside were the little things that made her real:

- A blue dupatta that still faintly smelled of her perfume
- A necklace she wore the day he told her he loved her
- A half-used diary with wildflowers drawn on the cover
- A photograph of them at the train station, both soaked in rain, both laughing like fools

His fingers trembled as he picked up the diary. He hadn't seen it in months. It was the same diary where she wrote her poems, her thoughts, her random late-night musings about the universe and love and what it meant to live.
He flipped to the last page she had written on.
Her handwriting sloped gently, hurried yet beautiful:
"Sometimes I wonder if memories have weight. Because the ones with you — they feel heavy. Not in a bad way. But like gravity. Like home."
Ronak closed the diary slowly, pressing it to his chest.
The room was still.
And then, as if guided by instinct, he reached into his drawer and pulled out a new pen — unused, unfamiliar. He opened his journal again, flipped past the ruined ink-blot

page, and began to write.

Not about the pain.

But about her.

"You hated the smell of wet socks. You always ate the cream layer of biscuits first. You cried during animated movies but laughed at horror ones. You loved old people and hated traffic. You said I looked like an owl when I was angry. You believed in signs, in stars, in impossible dreams. And somehow, you believed in me."

The words didn't stop.

They came like rain again — this time not a storm, but a cleansing drizzle.

He wrote until his wrist hurt, until the light outside dimmed into the warm hues of evening. He wrote until his heart felt raw but less suffocated.

And when he finished, he tore the page carefully and folded it.

He took it to the jasmine tree, dug a small hollow in the soil, and placed the note there gently.

"I'll write to you every day," he whispered. "Even if it's only one sentence. Even if it hurts."

The wind stirred the leaves above him — a soft, approving rustle.

And somewhere inside him, a voice answered.

Good. I'm still listening.

CHAPTER TWENTY-NINE

MEERA'S SILENCE

Ronak hadn't spoken to Meera in weeks.

It wasn't intentional. It wasn't because of anger, or bitterness, or anything dramatic. It was simply... silence. A thick, unspoken space that neither of them had dared to cross. And yet, she had been there — at Tarini's funeral, her eyes red-rimmed, her hands trembling as she lit a diya and whispered something to the flames.

Tarini and Meera had been inseparable since childhood — the kind of best friends who knew each other's moods through silence, who finished each other's sentences, who could sit in a room without saying a word and still feel full. Meera had been the first to know when Ronak and Tarini had started seeing each other. She had teased, poked, laughed, warned — and eventually, accepted. Fully.

She had once told Ronak, "Tarini feels safe with you. That's rare. Don't break her."

Now, Tarini was gone.

And both of them were broken.

That evening, Ronak stood outside Meera's house, unsure of what he was even doing there. The sun was bleeding orange into the sky, and the city around him buzzed with its usual indifference — car horns, chai stalls, dogs barking at the wind. But in his chest, there was only quiet.

He raised his hand to knock, hesitated.

And then the door opened.

Meera stood there in a simple kurti, her hair tied back, her eyes hollow. They stared at each other for a long time. No words. Just that deep, mutual ache, like a mirror reflecting back all the things they didn't know how to say.

"I was thinking about her," Ronak finally said.

Meera nodded, stepping aside to let him in. "So was I. I always am."

The house still smelled of Tarini's perfume. That surprised him — until he saw the bottle on the table.

Meera had placed it there like an offering.

"She forgot it here once," Meera said, noticing his gaze.

"I never returned it. Now I'm glad I didn't."

Ronak swallowed hard. "I broke the blue pen."

She blinked. "The one she stole from you?"

He nodded.

Meera managed a weak smile. "She loved stealing your things. You made it too easy."

They sat together on the floor — the same living room where Tarini had once danced around in her socks while Meera sang off-key Bollywood songs. The memories hung thick in the air. Every corner whispered her name.

"I haven't opened the letters yet," Meera said quietly.

Ronak looked up.

"She left me some too. Not twenty — just five. Said I didn't need as many because I already knew her better than she knew herself."

Ronak laughed. It came out broken, but it was laughter nonetheless. "That sounds like her."

"I read the first one," Meera said, "the day after we scattered her ashes. And then I couldn't bring myself to read the rest. I think... I was afraid it would make her feel more gone."

"Or more alive," Ronak murmured.

Silence settled again, but this time it wasn't painful.

It was shared.

Grief, they were learning, could be a bridge.

Meera stood suddenly and walked into her room, returning with a small velvet box — identical to Ronak's. She placed it between them and slowly lifted the lid.

The letters were there. Neatly stacked. Bound with a soft, red thread.

"Can we read one together?" she asked.

Ronak nodded, even as his chest tightened.

Meera pulled out the second letter and opened it with slow fingers. Her hands trembled slightly, but her voice was steady as she began to read.

Letter to Meera — "For the day the silence gets too loud"

Meera, my soul-sister,

I know you'll try to be strong. I know you'll smile at people, say "I'm fine," and then cry when you're alone. But please don't hide from the silence. Don't let it become your enemy. Let it teach you how to breathe without me.

And when it gets too loud, too sharp — call Ronak.

Even if you don't say a word. Just sit with him.

He carries my voice too. He'll understand.

I left you both with pieces of me. Maybe if you hold them together, you won't feel the weight as much.

Also — remember the blue saree I wore at your cousin's wedding? I buried my favorite earrings in your bookshelf.

Go find them, idiot.

I love you beyond words. I always will.

T.

Meera didn't speak after finishing the letter.

Her lips trembled. Her shoulders shuddered. But she didn't cry.

Instead, she reached for Ronak's hand.

He didn't pull away.

For a long time, they sat there, hands clasped tightly, surrounded by silence — the kind that no longer suffocated, but healed. Bit by bit. Scar by scar.

"She was right," Meera said finally. "You carry her voice too."

"So do you."

They both looked at the velvet box again.

Then at each other.

Maybe, Ronak thought, grief wasn't just about endings. Maybe it was about becoming a mosaic — broken, yes, but still whole in a different way. Maybe healing was learning to live with the cracks and letting light shine through them.

And maybe... just maybe, Tarini hadn't left them broken.

She had left them with enough pieces to build something new.

CHAPTER THIRTY

A SONG SHE NEVER FINISHED

The monsoon arrived late that year.

For weeks, the sky had teased the city with greying clouds and humid winds that offered no rain. But now, it poured — not in anger, but in waves of sorrow, as though the heavens themselves had caught the scent of Ronak's grief.

He sat by the window, his fingers tapping an old rhythm against the wood, one Tarini used to hum under her breath. The song had no lyrics. No beginning. No end. Just a tune she would whistle on slow afternoons, usually while stirring chai or scribbling lines in her diary. It had been her comfort tune — a lullaby she had composed without ever finishing.

He remembered asking her once, "What song is that?" She had laughed, brushing a strand of hair behind her ear. "I don't know yet. I'm still writing it. Maybe you'll finish it someday."

Back then, it had sounded like a flirt. Now, it felt like prophecy.

Ronak stood up abruptly. His fingers itched, his pulse racing with an urgency he didn't understand. He rummaged through drawers, under old papers and between half-filled notebooks, until he found what he was looking for — Tarini's guitar.

He hadn't touched it in months.

It was still tuned, surprisingly. Or maybe she had left it that way, knowing someone would come back to it. The strings were dusty, but when he plucked one, it hummed like her voice — soft, lingering, familiar. The weight of the guitar in his lap was almost unbearable. It was as though she had left a part of her soul behind in those strings.

He sat with it, cross-legged on the floor, the rain pelting the windows, thunder growling in the distance. And slowly, cautiously, he began to play.

The tune returned to him like a memory long buried — the exact notes she used to hum. It was in a minor key, full of longing. He followed it until the point where she always stopped, where the song would pause like a breath held too long.

He stared at that silence.

That unfinished space.

Then, he closed his eyes and played on.

The chords were rough at first, imperfect. But they carried weight. Emotion. Grief. Love. He let his fingers move without thinking, letting the ache in his heart guide them. As if Tarini was still there, beside him, nodding gently, whispering, "Yes. That's it."

He didn't know how long he played.

But when he finally opened his eyes, the song was done.

He wrote it down — every note, every change in tempo — and titled it **"Tarini's Rain."** He penned a few lines to go with it, not to fill the silence but to embrace it. It wasn't poetry. It wasn't even neat. But it was real.

Two days later, Meera visited.

She entered quietly, like she always did now, as if loudness would shatter something fragile in the air. She looked at him and then at the guitar resting against the wall. "You played it?" she asked.

He nodded.

"Can I hear it?"

He played it again.

She listened without speaking. Her eyes welled with tears, and by the final note, she was sobbing into her dupatta. The song echoed between them like a conversation spoken in another language — one made of memories, pain, and love.

"She would've loved it," Meera whispered. "She would've cried, and then made you play it again just to tease you. And then she'd say you stole her tune."

"She asked me to finish it," Ronak said, placing the guitar down gently. "And now it's done."

They sat in silence afterward, sipping chai Meera had made. Even the warmth of it felt like her. Cinnamon and cardamom — Tarini's favorite blend.

"I still talk to her," Meera said softly. "At night. Before sleeping. I tell her everything. It's stupid, but—"

"It's not stupid," Ronak interrupted. "I do too."

She smiled weakly, then looked at the sheet of music on the table. "We should record it."

Ronak raised an eyebrow.

"For her. For us. For the part of her that still exists in this world."

He considered it. The idea scared him — immortalizing the song meant acknowledging that Tarini was never coming back. But maybe that was the point. Maybe grief wasn't a prison — maybe it was a pilgrimage.

The next morning, they borrowed recording equipment from a friend. Meera handled the setup while Ronak practiced the melody again and again, fine-tuning every strum, every note.

When they recorded the final take, it was raining again. The sound of the rain wove itself into the music like a ghost.

They didn't edit it out.

They called the recording "Tarini's Rain — Final Cut" and uploaded it anonymously to a music-sharing site. No names. No explanation. Just a small note:

For anyone who has ever lost someone they couldn't imagine living without.

Within a few days, it had over ten thousand listens.

People left comments:

"This made me cry. I don't even know who Tarini is, but I miss her."

"Thank you for this. I lost my brother last year. This helped."

"I feel like this song knows how I feel."

Ronak read each comment. Every word was like a thread stitching him back together.

Tarini's memory wasn't fading.

It was expanding.

Touching strangers.

Helping them grieve.

Helping him live.

It wasn't just a song.

It was a heartbeat.

Hers. And his.

Still playing.

Still surviving.
Still loving.

CHAPTER THIRTY-ONE

LOST AT THE EDGE

The days blurred together, each one heavier than the last. The monsoon rains had come and gone, leaving the streets slick and glistening under the hesitant sunlight, but inside Ronak's small apartment, the air was thick with a silence that no storm could wash away.

It was not a peaceful silence. It was the silence of loss — a crushing, empty quiet that settled deep in his bones and echoed in every corner.

Ronak woke up each morning with the weight of it pressing down on his chest, an invisible hand squeezing tighter with every breath. The bed felt too big now, the sheets tangled around him like memories he couldn't untangle. On the bedside table, Tarini's favorite book lay untouched, the bookmark still stuck on the page where she had paused months ago.

He didn't know how to move forward.

The ache of her absence was a constant thrum beneath his skin. Her laugh, her voice, the way she scrunched her nose when she was thinking — all of it haunted him.

He often found himself staring at the empty chair by the window where she used to sit, her face lit by the soft glow of the afternoon sun, humming some tune only she knew.

Work had become a mechanical routine. His colleagues noticed his distracted eyes, the way he sometimes drifted mid-conversation as if listening to a distant echo only he could hear.

He didn't talk much. Talking felt pointless. How could words ever fill the void left by someone who was gone?

One rainy afternoon, as Ronak sat by the window with his guitar resting on his lap, his phone vibrated quietly on the table.

Meera.

Her name flashed on the screen. He stared at it, hesitating. She had been his lifeline since the accident — the friend who understood the weight he carried, the one who didn't ask him to pretend.

He finally answered.

"Ronak?" Her voice was soft but steady. "Can you come over? I think we need to talk."

He agreed, though his heart was heavy with uncertainty.

The streets were slick with rain, and the cool monsoon breeze brushed against his face as he walked to Meera's house.

The jasmine tree outside her window still bloomed, delicate white flowers perfuming the air, just as they had in happier days when Tarini's laughter filled the room.

Inside, the house was quiet, but charged with the weight of memories.

Meera led him to the living room, where the soft light filtered through curtains, casting gentle patterns on the floor.

Neither spoke for a while. The silence between them was not uncomfortable — it was the silence of shared pain.

Then Meera spoke, her voice breaking through the stillness.

"Do you remember the night before the accident?"

Ronak's throat tightened.

"Yes," he whispered.

"We were at the festival — the one Tarini loved so much. The colorful lights, the music, the smell of sweets in the air. She was radiant that night, full of life."

Ronak closed his eyes, the memory vivid as if it were yesterday.

Tarini dancing barefoot on the grass, her laughter mingling with the music, her eyes sparkling with a light that seemed untouchable.

"She pulled me aside after the fireworks," Meera continued. "She said she wanted me to tell you something."

Ronak's heart thudded painfully.

Meera's voice faltered, "She told me, 'Tell Ronak I love him. Tell him to never stop fighting — no matter what.'"

Tears welled up in Ronak's eyes, and he swallowed hard.

"I don't know how to fight without her," he admitted, his voice barely audible.

Meera reached out, taking his hand gently.

"Maybe fighting isn't about pretending you're okay," she said softly. "Maybe it's about living with the pain and still choosing to move forward — even when it hurts."

Ronak looked at her, the rawness of his grief laid bare.

"I feel so lost," he confessed. "Like I'm drowning in silence."

Meera squeezed his hand. "You're not alone."

They sat in the quiet together, two broken souls sharing the weight of a silence that had become too heavy to carry alone.

Outside, the sky began to clear, rays of sunlight breaking through the clouds.

For the first time in weeks, Ronak felt a fragile spark of hope flicker inside him.

Maybe healing wouldn't come all at once.

Maybe it would come in moments — in shared silences, in memories held gently, in the courage to keep living even when it felt impossible.

He picked up his guitar and played the tune Tarini had left unfinished.

The notes were shaky, imperfect, but filled with love.

And in that moment, Ronak realized that even in her absence, Tarini's song — their song — still lived on.

CHAPTER THIRTY-TWO

ECHOES OF A PROMISE

The monsoon had fully settled over the city. The air was thick with humidity, the sky heavy with dark clouds that threatened to burst again at any moment. But inside Ronak's small apartment, there was a different kind of storm — one of memories, regrets, and unspoken promises.

It was late evening. The only light came from the flickering lamp on the table, casting long shadows over the scattered pages of Tarini's diary, the unfinished lyrics she had scribbled, and the photo albums she had once filled with moments of joy.

Ronak sat cross-legged on the floor, the guitar resting on his knees, his fingers tracing the worn wood absently. It had been weeks since Tarini's death, but the pain felt as raw as the day he had received the call.

Sometimes he felt like screaming — screaming at the universe for taking her away, for stealing the warmth from his life. But instead, he sat in silence, drowning in memories that were both a comfort and a curse.

Tonight, something was different.

He opened Tarini's diary, the pages yellowed and soft from countless readings. Her handwriting was delicate, full of dreams and hopes that now seemed so distant.

One entry caught his eye — dated just a week before the accident.

"I want to go back to the little bookstore in Connaught Place. There's a collection of poems I've been wanting to buy for Ronak. He loves words the way I love music. Maybe someday, we'll open a small café together, with books and songs, where love won't be a secret."

Ronak's breath hitched. A café. A dream they had talked about in hushed tones, promising to build a life full of small joys — laughter over steaming cups of chai, evenings spent reading poetry, and music that never stopped.

He closed the diary slowly and looked around the room. It felt empty without her, but these memories were the only pieces left to hold onto.

Suddenly, his phone buzzed.

A message from Meera: *"Come over tomorrow. I found something you need to see."*

Curiosity sparked in him, and for the first time in days, he felt the faintest stir of hope.

The next afternoon, the skies threatened rain again as Ronak made his way to Meera's home. The jasmine flowers still bloomed, their scent drifting in the humid air. Meera opened the door with a soft smile, though her eyes were heavy with the same sorrow that mirrored his own.

"Come in," she said quietly.

In her living room, on the table, lay a small wooden box. Meera picked it up and handed it to Ronak.

"I found this among Tarini's things when I helped clean her room last week," Meera explained. "I think she wanted you to have it."

Ronak's hands trembled as he opened the box. Inside were letters, photographs, and a small, wrapped bundle.

He carefully unfolded the bundle to reveal a leather-bound journal — Tarini's personal journal, one he had never seen before.

His eyes scanned the cover: *"For Ronak — Our unfinished story."*

Over the next several hours, Ronak sat with the journal, reading Tarini's innermost thoughts and dreams. The pages were filled with her hopes for their future, reflections on their love, and her fears about the uncertain road ahead.

One passage stood out:

"Ronak, if you're reading this, it means I'm no longer there to hold your hand. But know this — my love for you is endless, and I want you to live fully, even when I can't be by your side. Promise me you'll find joy again, that you'll let yourself heal, no matter how long it takes."

Tears blurred Ronak's vision, but a quiet strength began to build within him.

Tarini had always been the light in his darkest moments, and now, even in death, she was guiding him forward.

In the days that followed, Ronak started to write again — letters to Tarini, unfinished songs, and reflections on their love. Meera became his anchor, visiting often and sharing stories about Tarini, helping him piece together memories.

One evening, as the rain fell steadily outside, Meera sat beside Ronak, who was strumming a new melody on his guitar.

"This song..." she whispered. "It's beautiful. It sounds like her."

Ronak nodded.

"She's still here," he said softly. "In every note, every word."

The pain of losing Tarini was still raw, but the echoes of her promise gave Ronak a fragile hope — that love, even lost, could still inspire, heal, and live on.

CHAPTER THIRTY-THREE

FRAGMENTS OF US

The days after Ronak received Tarini's journal blurred into a slow rhythm of memories and music. Each page he read brought him closer to her, yet reminded him of how painfully incomplete their story was.

Sometimes he would sit by the window for hours, watching the rain drip steadily, imagining Tarini's laughter breaking the monotony of the grey sky.

One afternoon, as he flipped through old photographs Meera had shared, a particular picture caught his eye. It was from the festival — the night before everything changed. Tarini's face shone with pure joy, her eyes sparkling under the fairy lights.

Ronak traced her smile with his finger, a bittersweet ache blooming in his chest.

"Why did you have to leave?" he whispered into the empty room.

Meera, sitting across from him, reached out gently.

"Because she loved fiercely," Meera said. "And sometimes, love is more about the moments we keep than the time we get."

Ronak looked up, tears welling in his eyes.

"I feel like I'm losing pieces of myself every day."

Meera nodded knowingly.

"Grief is like a puzzle. We lose pieces, but sometimes, new pieces come from memories, from those who loved her and loved you."

Inspired by Meera's words, Ronak began to reconnect with friends and family he had withdrawn from. They shared stories of Tarini's kindness, her fierce spirit, and her dreams.

Each story was a thread, weaving a tapestry of a life full of light and love.

One evening, Ronak visited the little bookstore Tarini had wanted to revisit — the one from her diary. The musty smell of old books and whispered pages brought a strange comfort.

He picked up a collection of poems, reading them aloud softly, imagining Tarini beside him, smiling.

There, among the bookshelves, he felt her presence — not as a ghost, but as the echo of the woman who had taught him how to love deeply, and how to carry that love even when she was gone.

The journey ahead was uncertain, but for the first time, Ronak felt ready to take the next step — to live a life that honored Tarini's memory, with every heartbeat echoing her name

THE QUIET STRENGTH

The monsoon had retreated, leaving behind a sky washed clean and a city waking slowly from its rainy slumber. But inside Ronak, the storm of grief was far from over. It had transformed, though — from a violent tempest into a quieter, more insidious ache that pulsed in the background of every thought and every breath.

He had begun to rejoin the world around him — meeting friends, visiting places that reminded him of Tarini, even returning to work with a tentative hope that time might dull the sharp edges of loss. But each day still carried the weight of her absence like an unspoken question: How do you live when half your soul is missing?

One evening, after a particularly long day at the office, Ronak sat alone on the rooftop of his building, gazing out at the glowing city lights that stretched into the horizon. The wind whispered softly through the leaves of the neem tree planted near the stairwell, carrying with it the faint scent of jasmine — Tarini's favorite flower.

He pulled out Tarini's leather-bound journal from his bag, the edges worn from his constant reading. He opened it to a page near the end, where she had written about strength — not the kind that shouts or storms, but the quiet, steady kind that holds everything together when the world feels like it's falling apart.

"Strength," her words read, *"is sometimes just surviving the day with a heart that feels like it's breaking, and still finding the courage to smile."*

Ronak closed the journal and pressed it to his chest, feeling the weight of her words settle deep within him.

A memory surfaced — the last time they had argued, just weeks before the accident. It was a silly disagreement over something trivial, but what he remembered most was how Tarini had looked at him afterward, her eyes soft but resolute.

"I love you, Ronak," she had said, voice steady. "No matter what happens, remember that."

He hadn't realized then how much those words would come to mean.

Now, sitting alone beneath the stars, Ronak understood the true meaning of quiet strength. It wasn't about fighting the pain or pretending it didn't exist. It was about letting the pain live alongside hope — allowing both to coexist, fragile but real.

The days that followed were filled with small steps. He reached out to his family more often, sharing memories of Tarini and listening to their stories of her kindness and laughter. He reconnected with old friends, letting their presence remind him that he wasn't alone.

Meera remained a constant support — a silent pillar of understanding. One afternoon, she invited Ronak to visit the little café she had started volunteering at, a cozy place filled with books and music, not unlike the dream Tarini had written about in her diary.

Walking through the doors, Ronak felt a strange comfort. The walls were lined with shelves of poetry and novels, the air fragrant with fresh coffee and rain-washed earth. Soft music played in the background — a guitar melody that made his heart ache and swell at the same time.

Meera smiled as she introduced him to the café owner, who welcomed Ronak warmly.

"This place feels like home," Ronak admitted quietly.

"Maybe it can be," Meera said softly. "A place to start again."

That evening, as he sat by the window sipping chai, Ronak thought of Tarini's words and the promise they had made — to build a life filled with love, music, and dreams.

He knew the path ahead would never be easy. The pain would return in waves, uninvited and relentless. But now, he also knew something else — that strength was not about erasing grief, but about living fully with it.

Under the gentle hum of the city, with the memory of Tarini lighting his heart, Ronak found a quiet strength rising within him.

A strength to face tomorrow, to keep her love alive, and to carry forward their unfinished story.

CHAPTER THIRTY-FIVE

A Step Into the Light

The morning sunlight spilled gently through the curtains of Ronak's apartment, casting soft patterns on the floor where dust motes danced lazily in the golden light. The world outside had begun to stir awake, but Ronak lay still for a long moment, his eyes tracing the familiar ceiling — the same ceiling he had stared at for endless nights filled with dreams of Tarini, and the unbearable weight of losing her.

Today was different, though. There was a quiet resolve in his heart, an ember that flickered stubbornly despite the heavy shadows of grief that clung to him.

He swung his legs off the bed and stood up, his feet touching the cool floor. The air was thick with the faint scent of jasmine, a reminder of Tarini's favorite flower and the countless times she had carried a bouquet home, her smile radiant and infectious.

Ronak moved to the window, pulling back the curtains to reveal the city awakening beneath a pale blue sky. The honking of autos, the chatter of street vendors, the distant hum of trains — all the familiar sounds of life continuing, relentlessly moving forward even when it felt like the world had stopped for him.

For months, Ronak had lived in a haze of memories and sorrow. The accident, the hospital, the funeral — each scene replayed in his mind like a cruel film he couldn't stop watching. His heart had broken into fragments, some so tiny they felt impossible to piece back together.

But today, for the first time, he felt the smallest flicker of something new. Not happiness, not quite, but a glimmer of hope. A fragile promise that maybe, just maybe, he could find a way forward.

He dressed quietly and stepped out into the soft morning. The streets were bustling as usual, vendors setting up their stalls, children laughing on their way to school, women chatting as they walked with their shopping baskets. The city breathed around him, alive and vibrant.

Ronak's destination was a small café tucked away in a quiet corner — a place Meera had recommended. She said it was special, filled with books and music, a sanctuary where people came to dream and create.

As he walked, his mind wandered to Tarini's journal, the letters she had written, and the dreams she had shared with him. He remembered her laughter, the way she had spoken about opening a café of their own — a haven of warmth and love where their souls could live on.

He wondered if she had imagined this moment — him taking a step out of the shadows, reaching for the light.

The café was exactly as Meera had described: cozy, filled with shelves of books, soft music playing in the background, the aroma of fresh coffee mingling with the scent of rain-damp earth. It was a place where time seemed to slow down, where stories lived in every corner.

Ronak took a seat by the window, watching the world outside as he sipped his chai. The warmth of the cup in his hands was grounding, a small comfort in the swirl of emotions.

A young woman approached his table with a smile. "You're Ronak, right? Meera told me you might come."

He nodded, surprised but grateful for the welcome.

"I'm Aisha," she said, setting down a plate of samosas. "I volunteer here. This place has helped me through a lot — maybe it can help you too."

Ronak smiled faintly, touched by her kindness.

They talked quietly, about the city, about books, about music. Aisha shared her own story of loss and healing, and for the first time in a long while, Ronak felt understood, seen.

Over the next few weeks, Ronak found himself returning to the café more often. He started to write again — poetry, letters to Tarini, fragments of songs that floated from his heart. The journal she had left him became his compass, guiding him through the tangled emotions.

Meera was a constant presence too, encouraging him gently, reminding him that healing was not a race but a journey.

One evening, as the sun dipped below the horizon, painting the sky in hues of orange and pink, Ronak sat on the rooftop of the café, guitar in hand. A small crowd had gathered, drawn by the music and the vulnerability in his voice.

He played a song he had written for Tarini — raw and beautiful, filled with pain and hope. As the final notes faded into the evening air, there was silence, and then applause.

Tears blurred Ronak's vision, but he smiled through them. For the first time, he felt like he was not just surviving — he was living.

That night, back in his apartment, Ronak sat surrounded by memories — photos, letters, the journal — and thought about the journey ahead.

He knew there would be dark days, moments when grief would threaten to consume him. But now, he also knew there was a quiet strength inside him, born from love and loss, that would carry him forward.

He closed his eyes and whispered a promise to Tarini's memory — to live fully, to love deeply, and to never forget the light she had brought into his life.

PART II

The Hollow Years

CHAPTER THIRTY-SIX

THE WEIGHT OF GOODBYE

The days grew shorter, the nights cooler as the season shifted imperceptibly. The city seemed to hold its breath, caught between the remnants of monsoon rains and the promise of dry autumn sunlight. But for Ronak, time had become a slow, heavy river—each day a long drift through the fog of his grief.

He sat alone in his apartment, the silence pressing down around him. The walls, once filled with Tarini's laughter and the warmth of their shared dreams, now echoed with absence. The photographs they had taken together, smiling and carefree, stared back at him from the shelves like ghosts of a life paused too soon.

The leather-bound journal rested on the table, its pages well-worn from his repeated readings. Tonight, though, he didn't want to open it. He felt the weight of memories pressing on his chest—too much to bear all at once.

Outside, the city pulsed with life, but inside Ronak, there was only a growing emptiness. The space where Tarini's presence had once been felt like an unfillable void.

He remembered the day of the accident with brutal clarity — the hurried phone call, the sterile hospital corridors, the finality of her last breath. It was a memory he had tried desperately to block out, but no matter how much time passed, it haunted him relentlessly.

Meera's words came back to him: *"Grief is a journey without a map. It twists and turns. You don't know what's ahead, only that you must keep moving."* But tonight, Ronak felt stuck. As if moving forward meant leaving Tarini behind — and he wasn't sure he could do that.

His fingers trembled as he picked up the phone. After several moments of hesitation, he dialed Meera's number.

"Ronak?" her voice was soft, cautious. "Are you alright?"

"I don't know," he admitted, voice breaking. "I feel like I'm drowning."

There was a pause, and then Meera said gently, "Come over. You don't have to face this alone."

The walk to Meera's house was shrouded in darkness, the streetlights casting long shadows on the quiet lanes. When Ronak arrived, Meera greeted him with a warm hug, and for the first time in days, he let himself lean on someone else's strength.

Inside, the small living room was cozy and filled with the scent of chai and sandalwood. Meera handed him a cup, and they sat in silence for a while, the shared quiet offering a small comfort.

Finally, Ronak spoke. "I don't know how to say goodbye," he whispered. "Not just to Tarini, but to everything we dreamed of. It feels like I'm losing her all over again."

Meera nodded, her eyes glistening with unshed tears. "Saying goodbye doesn't mean forgetting. It means

learning to live with the love, even when she's not here."
They talked late into the night, memories spilling forth like a river — stories of Tarini's laughter, her stubbornness, the way she had held Ronak's hand in moments of fear.
And then Meera said something that stayed with Ronak: "Grief changes you, but it also teaches you about the strength you never knew you had."
Over the following days, Ronak found himself trying to rebuild the fragile pieces of his life. He visited the little café again, where Aisha greeted him with her quiet smile. The music, the books, the gentle hum of life — they were reminders that even in loss, there could be moments of beauty.
One afternoon, as he sat strumming his guitar, a melody emerged — soft, aching, filled with the bittersweet memory of Tarini. He sang quietly, his voice raw but steady, the song a bridge between his sorrow and hope.
The café patrons listened with rapt attention, their eyes reflecting the emotion in his music. For the first time in a long while, Ronak felt a flicker of connection — not just to them, but to himself.
That evening, as twilight descended, Ronak returned home to find a letter slipped under his door. The handwriting was familiar — Meera's.
"Dear Ronak,
Sometimes the hardest goodbyes are the ones we never say. But in every ending, there is a new beginning waiting to bloom. Remember, you are not alone. You carry Tarini's love in your heart — and that love will guide you through the darkest nights.
With love and hope,
Meera."

Tears blurred Ronak's vision as he folded the letter carefully. It was a small light in the overwhelming darkness.

He looked up at the night sky outside his window, the stars distant but steady.

For the first time, he whispered aloud, "Goodbye, Tarini. And thank you."

The weight of goodbye was still heavy, but it was no longer crushing. It was a step — a painful, fragile step — toward healing. And with that step, Ronak felt, just for a moment, the possibility of peace.

CHAPTER THIRTY-SEVEN

ECHOES OF TOMORROW

The first light of dawn crept through the slats of Ronak's window blinds, spilling soft rays across the worn wooden floor. The air was cool and crisp—a gentle reminder that life moved in cycles, and with each new day came the faintest whisper of hope.

Ronak lay awake, eyes tracing the faint outlines of the ceiling fan slowly turning above him. His heart still carried the scars of loss, but somewhere deep inside, beneath the lingering shadows of grief, a quiet flame was beginning to glow.

He sat up slowly, the familiar ache in his chest still there but softened. Today was a day unlike the others — a day to step further into the world, to seek out the fragments of life that had survived the storm.

His phone buzzed beside him, and he picked it up with hesitant fingers. It was a message from Aisha, the kind soul he had met at the café — simple words, yet they lifted something inside him:

"Meet me at the gallery tonight. There's an exhibition opening. I think you'll like it."

A gallery. Art. Colors and emotions captured in frames and brushstrokes. It was a world Ronak hadn't visited since Tarini had been alive, but the invitation stirred a curious feeling — a mixture of nervousness and quiet excitement.

The day passed in a blur of ordinary tasks — work emails, calls, meals eaten in near silence. But Ronak's mind drifted to the evening, to the unknown waiting in that gallery space. Could art fill the emptiness? Could it help him weave new threads in the tapestry of his fractured heart?

As dusk settled, Ronak found himself standing before the entrance of a small but elegant art gallery nestled in a quiet street. The sign above read "Sparsh," a word meaning "touch" in Hindi — a fitting name for a place where emotions were painted and felt.

Inside, the gallery buzzed with soft murmurs, the clinking of glasses, and the faint scent of jasmine and sandalwood. Paintings adorned the walls — vibrant splashes of color, abstract shapes, and faces caught in moments of intense feeling.

Aisha spotted Ronak immediately and waved him over with a warm smile.

"Glad you came," she said softly, leading him deeper inside. "This exhibition is about stories — loss, love, healing. I thought it might resonate."

They moved slowly through the rooms, each painting telling a story that echoed fragments of Ronak's own journey. A canvas streaked with blues and greys reminded him of stormy nights spent in silence. Another, awash in golden light, spoke of hope rising from darkness.

Ronak paused before a large piece — a swirl of fiery reds and soft whites that seemed to dance and pulse with life. The plaque read: *"Echoes of Tomorrow"*.

He felt drawn to it, as if the painting was calling to him. In the chaotic beauty of colors, he saw the reflection of his own heart — broken but beating, fragile but fierce.

Later, as the crowd thinned and the gallery grew quiet, Aisha led Ronak to a small outdoor courtyard illuminated by string lights and lanterns.

"Music is next," she said, her eyes shining. "A few artists are performing. Would you like to join?"

Ronak hesitated, the familiar anxiety prickling his skin. But the warmth in Aisha's smile and the gentle rhythm of the evening urged him forward.

He took a deep breath and nodded.

The stage was small but intimate, surrounded by friends and strangers united by the shared language of art. When Ronak's turn came, he stepped forward with his guitar — an old friend and a companion in this journey through loss.

His fingers found the strings, and the first notes floated into the night air — soft, tentative, and full of raw emotion.

He sang a song he had written for Tarini, weaving their memories into melody and words. The lyrics spoke of love found and lost, of pain that cuts deep but cannot extinguish the light that love leaves behind.

As his voice carried into the cool night, Ronak felt a strange lightness — a feeling that maybe his grief was no longer a chain but a bridge.

The audience was silent, their faces reflecting the vulnerability and courage in his song. When the last note faded, the applause was warm and heartfelt.

After the performance, Aisha sat beside Ronak under the twinkling lights. "You were amazing," she said softly. "I think Tarini would be proud."

Ronak smiled, a bittersweet warmth blooming in his chest.

"Sometimes I wonder if she's still here, in moments like this," he confessed.

Aisha nodded knowingly. "She is. In the memories, the love, the art we create. She's in the echoes of tomorrow."

As the night wore on, Ronak and Aisha spoke about dreams — those Tarini had held close and the ones Ronak was beginning to dare to hope for again.

For the first time in a long while, Ronak felt the possibility of a future unfolding before him — a future where grief and love coexisted, where pain was not the end but a beginning.

When he finally walked back home under the quiet sky, his steps were lighter. The city hummed softly around him, full of life and promise.

At his apartment, Ronak sat by the window, gazing at the stars. He thought of Tarini — her laughter, her strength, her dreams. And he whispered into the night:

"I carry you with me, always. In every step, in every song, in every tomorrow."

The weight of loss was still there, but alongside it was something new — a fragile, beautiful hope that the echoes of their love would guide him into the light.

CHAPTER THIRTY-EIGHT

THE SILENCE BETWEEN US

Ronak woke to the muted light filtering through the thin curtains, the soft hum of the city seeping into his small apartment. His body ached—not just from the restless sleep, but from the invisible weight that grief had layered over his bones. Some mornings, the world felt impossibly heavy, as if every breath required more effort than the last.

He sat on the edge of his bed, hands folded in his lap, eyes fixed on the familiar space that had been both sanctuary and prison since Tarini's death. The quiet in the apartment was suffocating, yet strangely comforting. It was the silence between them—the silence that had grown after the accident—that pressed down on him most.

How do you speak to someone who is gone? How do you hold a conversation with a ghost?

His thoughts drifted back to the last days with Tarini—the way her eyes had shimmered with hope despite the pain, the softest touches she had left behind, the words never spoken. He remembered sitting by her bedside, his fingers entwined with hers, both trying to hold on and let go at once.

The silence between them was filled with unspoken promises, unfinished dreams, and a love that neither time nor death could erase.

The phone buzzed on the bedside table, pulling Ronak out of his reverie. It was Meera.

"Good morning," her voice was warm, a balm to his weary soul. "Are you coming to the support group today? It might help."

Ronak hesitated. He had been avoiding the group for weeks—partly because facing others who understood the depths of loss was painful, partly because he wasn't ready to share his silence with strangers. But Meera's kindness and gentle persistence softened his resistance.

"I'll come," he said quietly.

The community center where the group met was modest but inviting, filled with mismatched chairs arranged in a circle. Ronak took a seat near the back, the familiar scent of tea and old books comforting.

One by one, people shared their stories—their grief, their moments of despair, and the small sparks of hope that kept them going. Ronak listened, absorbing their pain and courage like water soaking into parched earth.

When it was his turn, his voice trembled as he began.

"I lost her... my Tarini," he said, swallowing the lump in his throat. "Sometimes, I feel like the silence she left behind is louder than anything I've ever known. It's in every room, every memory. It's in the space between my breaths."

He paused, the weight of his words settling over the circle. Tears streamed down his cheeks, and for the first time, he let himself break.

The group embraced his sorrow, their shared understanding weaving a fragile thread of connection.

After the meeting, Meera walked with Ronak to the nearby park. The evening air was cool and fragrant with blooming flowers. They sat on a bench beneath an ancient banyan tree, its sprawling branches a shelter from the world.

"Grief is like this tree," Meera said softly. "Its roots dig deep into the earth, anchoring us to the past. But its branches reach for the sky—toward new life and light. You have to let yourself grow, even if it means stretching into the unknown."

Ronak looked up at the tangled branches silhouetted against the darkening sky, feeling the truth in her words.

The days that followed were a slow, uneven climb. Some mornings, Ronak woke to hope; others, to despair. But he continued to write in Tarini's journal, to visit the café, to play his music in the spaces between silence.

One afternoon, as he wandered the city streets, he found himself drawn to a small temple tucked away behind a bustling market. The temple's walls were worn and ancient, its air thick with incense and prayer.

He stepped inside, the soft chants of devotees wrapping around him like a warm shawl. Ronak closed his eyes, folding his hands in silent prayer—not for a miracle, but for strength. For peace.

Weeks later, Ronak sat in the café once more, the place where his healing had quietly begun. Aisha approached with a tray of chai and samosas, setting them down beside him.

"Are you okay?" she asked, her eyes full of gentle concern.

Ronak nodded, a faint smile playing on his lips. "I'm getting there."

They talked about art, music, and the strange ways grief reshaped their lives. Aisha shared stories of her own losses, and Ronak felt the quiet power of shared understanding.

That evening, Ronak returned home and found a letter slipped under his door—a simple envelope with no name. Inside was a note in Tarini's handwriting, a letter he hadn't seen before.

"My dearest Ronak,

If you are reading this, it means you have found the strength to keep going. I want you to know that I am always with you—in every sunrise, every song, every breath you take. Please don't let my absence silence your heart. Live fully, love deeply, and carry our story forward.

Forever yours,

Tarini."

Ronak clutched the letter to his chest, tears streaming freely. The silence between them was no longer empty; it was filled with love, memories, and the promise of tomorrow.

That night, Ronak sat by the window, guitar in hand. He played softly, the music weaving through the quiet room, a melody of grief and hope intertwined.

In the silence between the notes, he heard Tarini's voice—not in words, but in the echo of their shared love. And for the first time in a long time, Ronak felt ready to listen.

CHAPTER THIRTY-NINE

DROWNING IN YESTERDAYS

The city around Ronak moved on as if nothing had changed. The cacophony of honking cars, the chatter of vendors selling their wares, the hurried footsteps of commuters—life carried on, indifferent to the quiet battle raging within him.

But inside Ronak, the world was fractured. Each piece a shard of memory, a fragment of love, a remnant of Tarini.

It had been months since her passing, yet the wound still ached as though fresh. He walked through his days wrapped in a fragile shell, each step a careful balance between holding on and letting go.

The morning began like any other, with Ronak sitting by the window of his apartment, a cup of chai cooling in his hands. The sky was overcast, the promise of rain hanging heavy in the air.

His eyes rested on the small box on the table—the one filled with letters, photographs, and keepsakes of their time together. He opened it slowly, running his fingers over the worn edges of a photograph of Tarini smiling, her eyes sparkling with mischief.

He smiled faintly, the bittersweet ache blooming in his chest. It was in these moments—alone with memories—that the weight of her absence pressed hardest. Ronak's phone buzzed, pulling him from his thoughts. It was a message from Meera.

"We're meeting at the park today. Would you like to come?"

He hesitated. The idea of facing others, of sharing space with those who carried their own grief, was daunting. But he knew isolation only deepened his pain.

After a moment, he replied, *"Yes, I'll be there."*

The park was alive with spring's arrival. Blossoms dotted the trees in soft pinks and whites, and the air was rich with the scent of earth and renewal.

The grief support group gathered beneath a sprawling banyan tree, the same one that had sheltered Ronak during his darkest days. Faces familiar and new greeted him with quiet smiles.

As the group began to share, Ronak listened to stories that echoed his own pain and hope—tales of loss, healing, and the courage to continue.

When his turn came, he spoke carefully.

"I carry her with me," he said, voice steady despite the tremor beneath. "In the silence, in the music, in the spaces we filled together. She's part of me now—every breath, every thought."

His words hung in the air, met with understanding and empathy.

After the meeting, Meera approached him.

"There's a project I'm working on—a memorial for those we've lost. It's a community art installation. Would you like to help?"

Ronak considered, then nodded. The idea of creating something tangible, something that honored Tarini and others like her, sparked a faint hope.

Over the following weeks, Ronak immersed himself in the project. He sculpted, painted, and wrote, pouring his grief into creation.

The installation took shape in the heart of the city—a mosaic of glass, stone, and light, reflecting the fragility and resilience of life.

On the day of the unveiling, Ronak stood beside Meera and others who had lost loved ones. The memorial shimmered under the afternoon sun, fragments of colored glass catching the light like scattered memories.

Ronak traced the edges with his fingers, feeling a quiet peace settle over him.

That evening, as he returned home, Ronak found a package on his doorstep. Inside was a journal—blank, waiting.

A note accompanied it, written in a delicate script: *"For your story. For the pieces of you that need to be told."*

It was from Aisha.

Ronak felt a surge of gratitude. He sat by the window, the journal open on his lap, and began to write—not just memories of Tarini, but of himself, of the journey through grief, and the fragments of love that remained.

Days turned into weeks, and the journal filled with words—pain and hope entwined on every page.

One morning, as Ronak walked through the bustling market, he heard a familiar laugh. Turning, he saw Aisha, her eyes bright and warm.

They talked beneath the shade of mango trees, sharing stories and dreams. Ronak felt the walls around his heart soften, the possibility of new beginnings gently stirring.

That night, Ronak played his guitar by the window, the melodies weaving through the quiet streets. His song was no longer just about loss—it was about life, love, and the courage to move forward.

As the last note faded, Ronak whispered into the night: "For every fragment of us, I carry your light."

And somewhere beyond the stars, he felt Tarini's presence — a gentle, eternal echo.

BENEATH THE MOONLIGHT

The moon hung low and full over the city, casting a silver glow that turned the streets into rivers of shimmering light. The night was quiet except for the distant hum of life — a soft lullaby for those who still carried the weight of the day in their hearts.

Ronak stood on the rooftop of his apartment building, wrapped in a thin shawl against the night's chill. His gaze drifted upward, tracing the pale outline of the moon as it slowly sailed across the sky. The quiet was different here — not empty, but filled with a gentle kind of presence.

Tarini's presence.

He closed his eyes, breathing in the cool air, feeling the pulse of the city below and the whisper of memories stirring in the silence.

It had been nearly a year since she was gone, but in the stillness of the night, her spirit felt as close as ever.

Ronak's journey through grief had been long and winding, filled with moments of despair and sparks of hope. Tonight, the loneliness was tempered by a fragile peace, a sense that he was no longer walking the path alone.

His phone vibrated softly in his pocket. Aisha's message appeared:

"There's a full moon festival in the park tonight. Music, dance, stories. Would you like to come?"

A flicker of hesitation sparked inside him, but he quickly typed back:

"I'll be there."

The park was alive with lanterns swaying gently in the breeze, their warm glow mingling with the soft light of the moon above. Music drifted through the air — rhythmic drums, haunting flutes, and the occasional burst of laughter.

Ronak moved through the crowd, feeling the pulse of life around him. Families sat on blankets sharing meals, couples danced beneath the trees, and children chased fireflies in gleeful abandon.

It was a celebration of life — a stark contrast to the emptiness he'd carried for so long.

Aisha found him near the center of the gathering, her eyes shining with excitement.

"I'm glad you came," she said softly. "Tonight, we celebrate those we've lost, but also the love that never fades."

Ronak nodded, the warmth of her presence comforting.

As the evening unfolded, stories were shared around a large bonfire. People spoke of their loved ones — their laughter, their dreams, the moments that defined them.

When it was Ronak's turn, he stood before the circle, heart pounding.

He began to speak, his voice steady but filled with raw emotion.

"Tarini was my light," he said. "Even in the darkest times, she shone so brightly. Losing her felt like losing the sun itself, but tonight, under this moonlight, I realize her light is still here — in the stars, in the music, in the love we shared."

Tears glistened in his eyes as he spoke, but there was no shame in them. Instead, there was a quiet strength — the strength born of love and remembrance.

After the stories, the music swelled, and people began to dance. Aisha took Ronak's hand gently, pulling him into the circle.

At first, his movements were hesitant, unsure. But as the rhythm took hold, his body relaxed, and he moved with a newfound freedom — a celebration of life rather than a mourning of loss.

They danced beneath the moonlight, the night sky wrapping around them like a protective cloak.

Later, as the festival wound down, Ronak and Aisha walked through the quiet paths of the park, the glow of lanterns fading into the first hints of dawn.

"I never thought I could find joy again," Ronak confessed. "But tonight... it feels like the world is opening up to me."

Aisha smiled, her eyes reflecting the pale light of morning.

"Grief changes us," she said softly. "But it doesn't have to define us. The love we carry shapes who we become."

As dawn broke, painting the sky in soft hues of pink and gold, Ronak felt a sense of renewal. The road ahead was still uncertain, but he no longer feared walking it.

He paused on the bridge overlooking the river, watching the water sparkle in the early light.

For a moment, he imagined Tarini beside him — her laughter echoing in the breeze, her hand warm in his. And though she was gone, her love remained — a constant flame beneath the moonlight, guiding him forward.

CHAPTER FORTY-ONE

ECHOES OF THE PAST

The morning sunlight filtered softly through the dusty windows of Ronak's apartment, painting the room in muted gold. The city was slowly waking—distant sounds of street vendors setting up their stalls, the faint murmur of conversations, and the rhythmic clatter of rickshaws navigating the narrow lanes below.

Ronak sat at his worn wooden desk, the same desk where, many months ago, he had first poured his soul into the pages of Tarini's journal. Today, the journal lay open before him, but the words seemed to blur, and the memories felt heavier than ever.

His fingers traced the delicate handwriting — Tarini's thoughts, dreams, and whispers preserved in ink. The pages were a lifeline, yet also a reminder of the void her absence had carved deep within his heart.

The day had been planned long ago but only now did Ronak feel ready. He was to visit Tarini's childhood home in a small village just outside the city, a place she had spoken of often but where he had never been.

The village was a world away from the relentless pace of urban life — narrow, winding lanes flanked by ancient banyan trees, houses painted in warm ochres and reds, and fields stretching toward the horizon like patchwork quilts.

As Ronak stepped out of the bus that had carried him here, the scent of jasmine and earth filled the air. Children played barefoot in the streets, their laughter mingling with the distant call to prayer from the village mosque.

He made his way to a modest home at the end of a lane lined with marigold flowers. The wooden door was chipped but sturdy, its frame decorated with rangoli patterns fading under the sun.

An elderly woman opened the door, her eyes widening in recognition the moment she saw Ronak.

"Are you... Ronak?" she asked, voice trembling.

He nodded.

"I'm Tarini's uncle," she said softly, stepping aside to welcome him in.

Inside the house, time seemed to slow. Photographs of Tarini as a child adorned the walls — smiling faces frozen in moments of joy. The furniture was simple but lovingly cared for, and the scent of fresh incense lingered in the air.

Ronak was led to a small courtyard where sunlight danced through the leaves of a neem tree. It was here Tarini had spent countless afternoons reading, dreaming, and playing.

Her uncle shared stories of her childhood — her curiosity, her laughter, and the fierce determination that had carried her through challenges.

"Tarini was always special," he said, eyes glistening. "Even as a child, she had a light that touched everyone she met."

As the day unfolded, Ronak felt the distance between them shrink. In the stories, the places, and the faces, he found pieces of Tarini he had never known.

He wandered through the fields she had once run through, imagining her bare feet brushing against the tall grass, her laughter carried on the wind.

The village held echoes of a life she had lived beyond the city — simple, vibrant, and full of love.

In the late afternoon, Ronak visited the local temple where Tarini had spent many mornings in quiet prayer.

The small shrine was decorated with fresh flowers and flickering oil lamps, the scent of sandalwood filling the air.

He sat on the temple steps, closing his eyes and letting the stillness wash over him.

For the first time since her death, he felt not just grief, but gratitude — gratitude for having known her, for the love they shared, and for the memories that would forever shape him.

As dusk settled, Ronak stood at the edge of a small pond near the village. The water mirrored the fiery hues of the sunset, casting ripples that danced like fragments of light.

He pulled from his pocket a folded letter Tarini had once given him—a letter he had been too afraid to read until now.

With trembling hands, he unfolded the paper.

"My dear Ronak,

If you are reading this, it means you are carrying me with you still. I want you to know that wherever I am, my love for you remains boundless.

Don't let my absence dim your light. Live fully, love deeply, and hold our memories close.

Always yours,

Tarini."

Tears blurred Ronak's vision as he folded the letter carefully and tucked it back in his pocket.

That night, Ronak stayed at the village guesthouse, the sounds of crickets and distant prayers lulling him into a restless sleep.

In his dreams, Tarini appeared—her smile radiant, her eyes filled with warmth.

They walked together beneath the stars, hand in hand, speaking without words.

When he awoke, the dawn was breaking, and with it came a renewed sense of purpose.

Returning to the city, Ronak carried the village's peace with him. The echoes of Tarini's past were now threads woven into his own story — fragments of love and loss, pain and hope.

He knew the road ahead would still be difficult, but beneath the weight of grief, a new strength was growing.

One born from memory, from love, and from the courage to face tomorrow.

CHAPTER FORTY-TWO

WHISPERS OF TOMORROW

The city was awakening once more, but for Ronak, the dawn felt different today — quieter, as if the world itself was holding its breath. The sunlight spilled through his apartment window in golden streaks, casting soft shadows on the scattered pages of his journal and the small keepsakes he had collected from his visit to Tarini's village.

He ran his fingers over a pressed marigold petal, fragile and yet enduring, a symbol of the love that lingered even in her absence.

Ronak's mind wandered to the letter Tarini had written — her words echoing in the quiet space between the ticking of the clock and the distant sounds of life beyond his walls.

"Live fully, love deeply, and hold our memories close."

Those words became a quiet mantra as he rose from his chair, ready to face the day with something he hadn't felt in months: hope.

He decided to visit the old bookshop where he and Tarini had spent countless afternoons. The small store was tucked away in a narrow alley, its wooden sign swaying gently in the morning breeze.

The bell above the door jingled softly as Ronak stepped inside. The scent of aged paper and polished wood enveloped him, a comforting reminder of simpler times.

At the counter stood Mr. Sharma, the elderly shopkeeper, who greeted Ronak with a knowing smile.

"Back again, Ronak? Your visits bring a bit of life to this quiet place."

Ronak smiled faintly. "I come here to remember."

They talked for a while about books, memories, and the passage of time. Mr. Sharma listened patiently as Ronak spoke of Tarini, of her love for poetry and her endless curiosity.

Before Ronak left, the shopkeeper handed him a small, wrapped package.

"For you," he said. "Something she wanted you to have."

At home, Ronak carefully unwrapped the package. Inside was a beautifully bound collection of poetry — Tarini's favorite poet, Kabir.

A handwritten note fell from between the pages:

"For Ronak — may these words guide you through the shadows."

Ronak held the book close, feeling as if Tarini's hand had reached across time to touch his heart.

Inspired, Ronak began to write again — poems, letters, and fragments of their story woven together in a tapestry of grief and love.

His writing became a balm, a way to transform sorrow into something enduring.

He shared his work with Aisha, who encouraged him to consider publishing it someday.

"You have a gift," she said gently. "Your words can help others who are lost in their own darkness."

One afternoon, as the monsoon rains began to fall softly outside, Ronak received a call from Meera.

"We're organizing a community event — a day to honor those we've lost and to celebrate the strength it takes to move forward. Would you like to read something?"

Ronak hesitated, then agreed. The thought of standing before others, sharing his pain and hope, felt daunting but necessary.

The day of the event arrived with skies heavy and gray. The park was filled with familiar faces — friends from the support group, neighbors, and strangers bound by shared loss.

Ronak's heart raced as he stepped onto the small stage, clutching his notebook tightly.

He began to read, his voice steady and filled with emotion.

His poems spoke of love that transcended death, of the fragile beauty in pain, and the quiet courage of those who keep living despite the ache.

The crowd was silent, tears glistening in many eyes, their hearts echoing the truths in his words.

Afterward, people approached him with gratitude, sharing their own stories and thanking him for giving voice to what they felt but could not say.

Ronak realized then that his grief was no longer a solitary burden — it was a thread that connected him to others, a bridge between hearts.

That evening, as the rain softened to a drizzle, Ronak walked along the riverbank, the city lights shimmering on the water's surface.

He thought of Tarini — her laughter, her dreams, the warmth of her hand in his.

Though she was gone, her whispers filled the night, urging him to keep moving forward.

"To live is to carry love into the future," he whispered to the wind.

Under the vast sky, Ronak felt a quiet resolve taking root within him — a promise to honor Tarini's memory by embracing life's fragile, fleeting beauty.

The past would always be a part of him, but so too would be the hope of tomorrow.

CHAPTER FORTY-THREE

CROSSROADS OF THE HEART

The days had begun to fold into one another, an endless stream of gray skies and soft rain. The monsoon had arrived, drenching the city with relentless showers, washing the streets clean but stirring old memories within Ronak's heart. Every raindrop seemed to echo the tremors of his soul, carrying whispers of Tarini's laughter and the warmth of her touch.

Ronak stood by the window of his small apartment, watching the rain blur the bustling world outside. The city was alive with motion, but inside him, a storm brewed—a tempest of grief, hope, and uncertainty.

Since the event in the park, Ronak had felt a subtle shift inside. The first stirrings of healing, mingled with the ever-present ache of loss. The poems he wrote became a bridge between what was and what might be.

But life had begun to press on in unexpected ways. Aisha had become a steady presence — a gentle light in the shadowed corners of his days. Her kindness was a balm, her laughter a reminder that joy could still exist, even amid sorrow. Yet, Ronak found himself torn, caught between the memory of Tarini and the possibility of a future he never dared imagine.

One rainy afternoon, Ronak received a call from Aisha. "Would you like to come over? I made chai," she said with a warmth that reached across the phone.

The invitation felt like a lifeline. He accepted.

At Aisha's apartment, the air was fragrant with spices and the comforting aroma of fresh tea. They sat by the window, watching the rain paint silver trails down the glass.

For a while, they spoke of everything and nothing — the little moments that made life meaningful. The city, their favorite books, and the strange way grief could sometimes bring people closer.

Then, gently, Aisha asked, "How are you, really?"

Ronak paused, searching for words that could capture the storm inside him.

"I'm learning," he said finally. "Learning how to live again without her."

Aisha reached out, her hand resting lightly over his.

"You don't have to do it alone."

That evening, Ronak walked home beneath the rain, the cool droplets soaking through his clothes but failing to dampen the quiet hope blossoming inside.

The city felt different now — less like a place of endings and more like a crossroads.

Over the next few weeks, Ronak and Aisha's friendship deepened. They shared meals, stories, and laughter, building a fragile trust that began to heal the fractures in Ronak's heart.

Yet, with each step forward, the ghost of Tarini lingered — in the quiet moments, in the spaces between words, and in the night's solitude.

Ronak found himself torn between the past and the future, love remembered and love renewed.

One evening, as the monsoon rains softened to a gentle drizzle, Ronak sat alone in his room, staring at a photo of Tarini. Her smile was a beacon, but it also cast long shadows.

He whispered to the empty room, "Can I love again? Without betraying you?"

The silence that answered was heavy but honest.

Days later, Ronak met Meera at a café. She had been a friend through the darkest times, a voice of reason and compassion.

"Ronak," she said softly, "love isn't a zero-sum game. Loving again doesn't mean forgetting."

Her words settled over him like a balm, easing the knot of guilt he carried.

The city around them thrummed with life and possibility. As the monsoon rains finally began to ease, the first rays of sunshine pierced the clouds, casting warm light on the wet streets.

Ronak felt the stirrings of something new — a tentative hope, fragile yet real.

At Aisha's suggestion, they took a walk through a nearby garden. The earth was fresh, the flowers bright and wet with rain.

As they strolled beneath the trees, Ronak realized the path ahead was not a straight line but a winding road — full of turns, pauses, and unexpected beauty.

He turned to Aisha and smiled, the weight in his chest lightening for the first time in months.

That night, as Ronak lay in bed, the city quiet except for the distant hum of life, he felt a whisper on the breeze — a promise that love, in all its forms, could heal even the

deepest wounds.
Tarini's memory remained, a guiding star. But Ronak knew he was ready to step forward, to embrace the uncertain but hopeful dawn.

CHAPTER FORTY-FOUR

A FLICKER OF HOPE

The city had finally emerged from the relentless monsoon. The rain had ceased, leaving behind a fragile freshness in the air — a quiet promise that even after the darkest storms, life could begin anew. The sun's golden rays touched the streets with gentle warmth, but for Ronak, the morning light felt fragile, as if it could shatter with the slightest pressure.

He stood by the balcony window of his apartment, the cool breeze ruffling his hair, carrying distant sounds of life — the laughter of children, the honking of vehicles, the clinking of cups in a nearby chai stall. The world was moving forward, but inside him, a war waged between the past and what lay ahead.

Tarini's memory was a constant shadow, lingering in every corner of his mind. It was not just the absence of her presence but the vividness of what had been — the way her eyes lit up with dreams, the softness of her voice whispering promises of forever. The pain of losing her was a raw wound, one that refused to heal but throbbed with every heartbeat.

The weeks since the park event — where Ronak had bared his soul in poetry — had been a rollercoaster of emotions. The outpouring of support had been overwhelming, yet the comfort of strangers could never replace the warmth of Tarini's hand in his.

Aisha's gentle presence had become a lifeline. She was patient, never rushing him, never demanding more than he could give. Yet, even as they grew closer, Ronak's heart was shackled by guilt.

Could he open himself to love again without betraying the memory of the woman who had been his everything?

That morning, after the first cup of tea, Ronak decided to visit the park — the place where countless memories of Tarini had been made. The path was still damp from the rain, the earth smelling of wet leaves and fresh beginnings.

He found their favorite bench beneath the sprawling branches of the peepal tree. It was here that Tarini had once confided her dreams, her fears, and the promise that no matter what happened, they would face life side by side.

Ronak sat down slowly, the wood cold against his palms. Opening Tarini's poetry book, he traced her favorite verses with trembling fingers. Her handwriting, delicate and looping, felt like a whisper from the past.

Lost in the poetry, he almost didn't notice a soft voice behind him.

"Ronak?"

He looked up to see Meera, her eyes filled with concern and something deeper — understanding.

"Meera," he said, rising to greet her.

They walked together through the garden, the flowers heavy with droplets, their fragrance mingling with the earthiness of the wet soil.

Meera was quiet at first, letting the silence hold the space between them.

Finally, she spoke softly, "How have you been holding up?"

Ronak's voice cracked. "Some days are better. Others… I feel like I'm drowning all over again."

Meera stopped and turned to face him. "You don't have to carry it alone."

Her words were a balm, but the pain in Ronak's chest remained a heavy weight.

"I'm afraid of forgetting her — or worse, forgetting what she meant to me."

"Loving someone new doesn't erase the love you had," Meera said gently. "It adds layers. Your heart isn't a container that runs empty. It expands."

Ronak wanted to believe her, but the fear was real — that moving forward might mean leaving Tarini behind.

Later that afternoon, Ronak called Aisha. Hearing her voice was like a warm embrace — steady and kind.

They met at their usual café, a quiet place tucked away from the city's noise. Over steaming cups of chai, their conversation flowed like a gentle river, carrying away the weight of the day.

Aisha reached across the table, her hand brushing his. "Sometimes, it's okay to let yourself feel happy again," she said.

Ronak swallowed the lump in his throat, eyes searching hers. "I want to. But I'm scared."

Scared of what? Of losing Tarini's memory? Of breaking under the weight of hope?

Aisha squeezed his hand. "We'll take it one step at a time. No rush."

Days passed, each one weaving threads of healing and doubt. Ronak found himself writing again — not just about grief, but about the faint light flickering at the edge of his sorrow.

His poems were messengers, fragile yet persistent, carrying the truth that pain and hope could coexist.

One evening, Ronak found himself volunteering at a shelter where Aisha worked. The shelter was a refuge for those broken by life's cruelty — women, children, men who had nowhere else to turn.

He saw their stories reflected in his own — pain, loss, the struggle to find meaning.

Helping them gave his grief a purpose. In their smiles and tears, he found pieces of himself he thought were lost forever.

As the sun dipped low, Ronak walked home beneath a sky painted with fiery hues of orange and pink. The city lights flickered to life, mirroring the tiny embers of hope glowing in his heart.

He paused at a rooftop garden overlooking the river, the water shimmering in the twilight.

He closed his eyes and breathed deeply.

"I miss you," he whispered into the wind. "But I'm trying. For you. For me."

That night, sleep was elusive. His dreams were a tapestry of memories — moments of joy with Tarini, the pain of her loss, and glimpses of a future he dared not fully imagine.

Morning came with a hesitant light.

The next day, Ronak and Aisha took a long walk through the city's old neighborhood — the narrow lanes where life bustled with the messy beauty of everyday existence.

They stopped at a small street vendor selling bright marigolds — the same flowers Tarini loved.
Ronak picked a handful, inhaling their scent, feeling a bittersweet connection.
As they walked, Aisha shared stories of her childhood, her dreams, and her fears.
Ronak listened, heart opening to the possibility of new stories — stories where Tarini's memory was honored but did not imprison him.
Underneath the vast sky, with the city alive around them, Ronak realized that healing was not about forgetting, but about weaving the past into the fabric of the future.
His heart was fragile, cracked by loss but still beating with the fierce hope that love, in all its forms, could endure.
In the quiet moments before sleep, Ronak held Tarini's poetry book close.
A flicker of hope burned softly within him — a promise that even in the darkest nights, dawn would come.
And with it, the courage to love again.

CHAPTER FORTY-FIVE

THE SKY FORGOT HER TOO

The silence in the room was suffocating. It wasn't the kind of silence that offered peace, but the kind that pressed heavily on Ronak's chest, squeezing the breath from him with every heartbeat.

Tarini's absence was no longer just a hollow space in his life—it had become an unbearable weight that bent him, twisted him in ways he hadn't thought possible.

The world outside moved with its usual noise and color, but inside his small apartment, time had slowed to a crawl. The walls seemed to close in, trapping him in memories he couldn't escape, and feelings he couldn't undo.

It had been months since Tarini's death, but the wound felt as fresh as the day the news had shattered his world. He still remembered the phone call—the frantic voice on the other end, the sirens, the blaring hospital lights, the cold sterility of the ICU.

He remembered the way her hand had slipped from his grasp, the soft whisper of her name, and the silence that followed.

No matter how many days passed, that silence echoed inside him—louder than any cry, sharper than any scream.

Ronak sat on the floor, surrounded by remnants of their life together. Old letters tied with a faded red ribbon, photographs with smiles frozen in time, Tarini's favorite scarf, still carrying the faint scent of jasmine.

His fingers trembled as he picked up a letter she had written during their last trip to the mountains — her words filled with hope, dreams of a future they had planned but would never live.

His eyes blurred with tears.

"Why did you leave me, Tarini?" he whispered, voice breaking.

The answer was nowhere to be found.

Aisha's voice was soft when she came in, hesitant as if afraid to disturb the fragile cage around him.

"Ronak... you don't have to do this alone."

He looked up, eyes red and hollow.

"How do I let go, Aisha?" he asked, his voice raw. "How do I say goodbye to someone who is still living in every breath I take?"

Aisha sat beside him, her hand reaching out to cover his.

"Grief doesn't ask for permission. It doesn't have a timetable," she said gently. "You carry her with you — in your heart, in your memories. Saying goodbye doesn't mean forgetting."

Ronak shook his head. "It feels like forgetting is the only way to survive. But how can I forget her? She was my everything."

Aisha's eyes glistened with tears she refused to shed. "You don't forget. You learn to live with it. To find moments of peace in the storm."

The days blurred into one another. Sometimes Ronak found himself awake in the middle of the night, staring at the ceiling, his mind trapped in an endless loop of 'what ifs' and 'if onlys.'

What if he had noticed the signs earlier? What if he had held her tighter? What if she had survived?

The questions were cruel ghosts, tormenting him with their relentless presence.

One evening, Ronak stood by the riverbank, the city lights shimmering like distant stars. The water reflected his troubled face, distorted by ripples, as if the universe was mocking his pain.

He whispered to the night, "I don't know how to move on without you."

The wind stirred, cold and indifferent.

But even in the depths of his despair, there were moments — fragile, fleeting — when Tarini's love seemed to reach through the darkness.

A memory would flash — her laughter, the way she looked at him when she thought he wasn't watching, the soft touch of her hand on his cheek.

Those moments were both a balm and a blade, healing and hurting all at once.

Ronak realized that grief was not a destination, but a journey — one that would reshape him forever.

He started to write again, pouring his pain and love into his poetry. The words were jagged, raw, and honest — a testament to the storm inside him.

Writing became a way to keep Tarini alive, to speak to her when the world was too silent.

One afternoon, Aisha brought him a letter.

"It's from Tarini's mother," she said quietly.

Ronak's hands shook as he opened the envelope. Inside was a letter filled with love, sorrow, and a plea for him to find peace.

Her mother wrote of Tarini's dreams, her wishes for Ronak, and how deeply she believed that Tarini wanted him to live fully — to love and be loved again.

The letter became a turning point.

Ronak understood that holding on to grief was not honoring Tarini's memory. It was chaining himself to a pain that would consume him.

Slowly, painfully, he began to let go.

The process was not linear. There were days he felt strong, and days when the weight of goodbye crushed him anew.

But in those moments of weakness, he found strength in Aisha's presence, in the support of friends, and in the enduring love that Tarini had left behind.

One night, under a sky filled with stars, Ronak whispered to the darkness:

"I will carry you with me, Tarini. Always. But I will learn to live again."

A tear slid down his cheek — not of despair, but of release.

The weight of goodbye was heavy, but in letting go, he found the flicker of hope that would guide him forward.

CHAPTER FORTY-SIX

THE ECHO IN HER WALLS

The journey back to Tarini's childhood home in Dehradun was not planned. Ronak had stumbled across an old, worn-out envelope tucked in the pages of one of her books — *"A House Full of Sunlight"*. It was her favorite. The envelope contained a faded photograph of her as a child standing beside a bougainvillea bush, her face lit up by a smile so wide it seemed to glow. On the back, in her neat handwriting, were the words:

"The house that raised me, the roots that made me."

That one line was enough. Two days later, he found himself on a bus bound for Dehradun, carrying nothing but a small bag and a heart heavy with memories.

The hills rolled past him like silent witnesses. The scent of pine and earth reminded him of her—how she would always talk about wanting to retire to the hills someday, raise dogs, and paint in a little studio that overlooked a valley.

She used to joke, *"Ronak, I'll paint you every day until you get tired of yourself."*

But life hadn't waited long enough for the paint to dry.

The house stood at the end of a quiet lane, flanked by moss-covered stone walls and a rusting green gate. The bougainvillea still bloomed wildly, a chaos of color tangled in branches. He stood frozen for a long moment before finally pushing the gate open. It creaked like an old memory.

The woman who answered the door was her aunt—Anjana. She hadn't seen Ronak in years, but when she looked into his eyes, her own filled with tears.

"You've come," she whispered. "I always thought you would."

Ronak bowed his head slightly, his voice lost in the lump in his throat.

Inside, nothing had changed.

The wooden swing in the living room still creaked softly in the breeze. The walls bore the same framed paintings Tarini had done in school—rivers, butterflies, a crooked tree in bloom. Her room upstairs had been left untouched, a shrine to her youth.

Ronak stepped in alone.

The room smelled faintly of lavender and dust. Her desk was cluttered with pens, notebooks, tiny drawings on yellowed pages. On the wall, photographs of her younger self grinned back at him: Tarini with a birthday cake, with her bicycle, with a book nearly bigger than her head.

There was one photo of them together — the day he had met her family for the first time. He had on a silly shirt, and she had teased him for weeks.

He sat on the edge of her bed, staring at the photo until his hands trembled.

He found a box beneath her bed. Inside were things she had never told him about.

A journal. Letters addressed to her future self. A list of places she wanted to go — *"before I turn thirty,"* she had written.

He read her journal late into the night under a dim lamp. Her words were fireflies dancing through the dark: *"Sometimes I'm scared that I feel too much. That this world might not be built for people like me. But then I look at Ronak, and I think — maybe love is the armor."*

He clutched the notebook to his chest, trying to keep the shards of his heart from spilling.

In the morning, Anjana served him parathas and tea, her voice quiet as the ticking of the clock.

"She used to sit right there," she said, nodding to the chair opposite him. "Every morning, singing to herself. She was a river that didn't know it was made to flood everything around her."

Ronak's eyes welled up again. "Why did she have to go, Anjana Mausi?"

Her hands gripped the edge of the table. "Some lives burn too bright to last long."

Before leaving, Ronak walked to the back garden. The swing Tarini had often mentioned in her stories was still tied to the old banyan tree. He sat on it, gently swaying, staring at the mountain line in the distance.

He closed his eyes and imagined her there—barefoot, laughing, arms open wide like she was trying to hug the whole sky.

He whispered into the breeze, "I came, Tarini. I saw the world you grew in. I heard the walls echo with your laughter. I felt you everywhere."

A gust of wind rustled the leaves above him, and for a fleeting second, it felt like she was near.

That night, as he boarded the bus back to the city, he felt like he was leaving her behind all over again.

But deep down, he knew — he wasn't returning with empty hands. He was bringing her memories, her dreams, and the whisper of her childhood laughter carved into his soul.

She wasn't gone.

Not entirely.

She had simply become the house inside him.

And now, he carried her with him wherever he went

CHAPTER FORTY-SEVEN

LETTERS TO THE MOON

The city welcomed Ronak back with its usual chaos — honking cars, restless footsteps, and neon signs blinking against the darkness. But Ronak moved through it like a shadow, half-present, half-lost in the weight of everything he carried from Dehradun.

Tarini's journal was now his most precious possession. He read a few lines every night, like a prayer. Her handwriting, so alive and fluid, gave him the illusion that she was still speaking to him, whispering thoughts she never had the chance to say aloud.

But the silence in his heart remained vast — a void too large for words alone.

So, he began to write.

The first letter was simple.

Dear Tarini,

It's been 143 days. I count them, not because I want to — but because I can't help it. Every day without you feels like a stone added to my chest. I went to your childhood home. I sat on the swing you told me about. I think I heard your laughter in the wind.

I miss you in ways I don't know how to express. I hope you're looking at the moon, wherever you are.

Love,

Ronak

He folded the letter, placed it in an envelope, and addressed it to nowhere.

Then he went to the rooftop and tied it to a white helium balloon. As the balloon lifted into the night sky, dancing against the stars, he whispered:

"Find her."

It became a ritual.

Every night, Ronak would write a letter — sometimes a memory, sometimes a regret, sometimes just a word: *Why?*

He sent a balloon into the sky with each letter.

Neighbors began to wonder about the young man who spoke to the stars, who cried quietly on his rooftop, who released his heart into the sky night after night.

They didn't understand.

But he didn't need them to.

Because with every letter he sent, he felt a little lighter — like grief was a heavy rain, and his love for her was becoming wings.

One evening, while sorting through an old drawer, Ronak found the sketch Tarini had once made of him — unfinished, hastily folded. His face was only half-complete, but her detailing was delicate, loving. She had drawn his eyes with such care, as though she had studied them for years.

He stared at it for a long time.

Then he picked up a pen and, with trembling fingers, completed it.

It didn't match her style. It wasn't perfect. But it was theirs.

He placed the drawing inside his next letter.

Dear Tarini,

I finished the sketch you started. I hope you don't mind. It's the only way I know how to keep building the life we didn't get to finish.

I'll keep drawing, even when my hands shake.

Because you taught me how to create beauty from pain.

Always yours,

Ronak

Aisha visited again.

She had been giving him space, checking in with quiet texts, soft encouragements. But this time, she arrived with two cups of chai and a notebook.

"I want you to write something for the literature magazine," she said, placing the notebook on his table. "An essay. Or a letter. Or... whatever you feel. I think people need to hear your story."

Ronak looked away. "It's not a story. It's just... broken pieces."

"Exactly," she said gently. "That's why it matters."

That night, he stared at the blank page for hours.

And then he wrote.

The world tells us to move on. But no one tells us how to carry the love that no longer has a hand to hold.

No one tells you how loud the silence gets. Or how certain songs become weapons. Or how grief becomes a second skin. But maybe... maybe it's okay to carry love with grief. Maybe they are two sides of the same heart.

He submitted it under the title: *"Letters to the Moon."*

Days later, Aisha called, voice shaking with emotion.

"Your piece... it's being shared everywhere. People are crying. They're writing their own letters now. You've started something, Ronak."

He didn't know what to say.

He had only written for her.

And yet, somehow, Tarini's memory was now touching hundreds of strangers. Her story, their love, was no longer buried — it was blooming.

That night's letter read:

Dear Tarini,

They're writing too. People I'll never meet are writing letters to the ones they lost. Maybe you already know. Maybe you're reading them from where you are.

Your love has become a lighthouse.

And somehow... I think I'm learning how to breathe again.

Yours,

Ronak

As the balloon disappeared into the dark, Ronak smiled — not because the pain had lessened, but because he had found purpose in the ache.

She had not left him entirely.

She had simply become the voice inside his soul, the ink in his pen, and the light in the dark.

CHAPTER FORTY-EIGHT

THE PLACES WE PROMISED

The old map lay unfolded on Ronak's bed — creased at the edges, some names nearly faded. Tarini had marked their dream destinations with little red hearts. It was something they had made together during one of those giddy late-night conversations, when the world felt small and love felt endless.

"I want to see every place with you," she had said, twirling her pen. "Let's write our own story across the sky."

He traced the red hearts with a fingertip now trembling.

Jaipur. Udaipur. Rishikesh. Pondicherry. And somewhere near the bottom: "And one day... Paris."

He couldn't go to Paris. Not yet. But he could try the others.

For her.

Ronak packed lightly: a backpack, her journal, his letters, and the map. The journey wasn't about sightseeing. It was about chasing echoes, collecting memories they never made, whispering her name into the wind where she had once dreamed of standing.

His first stop was Rishikesh.

He stayed in a quiet ashram by the river. Tarini had always wanted to learn yoga there, to wake up with the sun and sleep to the sound of the Ganga's lullaby.

On the first morning, he woke at dawn, walked barefoot to the banks, and sat cross-legged near the water. He closed his eyes and whispered a line from one of her poems:

"In rivers, I leave pieces of myself — flowing, free, forgiving."

He stayed still for hours, breathing with the rhythm of the river.

He dipped her photo in the water and let it drift — not to forget, but to release. To allow her spirit to move beyond the pain.

In Udaipur, he watched the sunset from the palace lakeside — the same view Tarini had saved as her phone wallpaper for years.

The wind was cold that evening. He sat on the marble steps by Lake Pichola, writing in her journal:

Dear Tarini,

I sat where you wanted to sit. I watched the sunset you dreamed about. And all I could think was — why weren't you here to see it?

But maybe... maybe you are. Maybe this breeze brushing my cheek is your laugh. Maybe this golden sky is your smile.

I miss you. Always.

Love,

Ronak

He folded the note and tucked it under a loose tile in the wall behind him, hiding a piece of their love in the city she once loved from afar.

Jaipur was filled with noise, colors, and crowds — overwhelming, but oddly comforting. Tarini had always said she wanted to shop in its bazaars, wear silver anklets, and eat kulfi on a hot afternoon.

So, Ronak did it all.

He wandered through Johari Bazaar, buying a silver anklet and placing it in his pocket. He ordered kulfi and sat on the edge of a quiet bench, letting the syrupy sweetness linger on his tongue.

A little girl walked past him wearing bangles, laughing like wind chimes.

He looked up at the sky, fighting the sting in his eyes.

"She would have loved this moment," he whispered.

Back at his rented guesthouse, he stared at the map again. One red heart remained within reach: Pondicherry.

He hesitated.

It was the last place they had marked before life took a turn. It felt like the final thread holding their plan together.

Would going there sever it completely?

Or... would it be a beginning?

The train to Pondicherry was long and winding. He watched the scenery shift from dry plains to coastal greens, clutching Tarini's journal the entire way.

When he arrived, the air smelled of salt and jasmine. The French quarters were painted in pastel yellows and blues, the roads narrow and quiet, the sea not far behind.

He found a spot near the promenade at sunrise.

Tarini's last entry in the journal read:

"One day, we'll watch the sea in silence, and know everything we need to."

So he sat in silence. For hours. Watching the waves come and go, like breath, like time.

He spoke no words. He didn't need to.
Somewhere in the sound of the ocean, he heard her
voice again.
That night, he lit a paper lantern by the beach. He tied
to it the final letter from this journey:
Dear Tarini,
I went to every place we promised. I carried you with me,
in my steps, in my sighs, in every sunset.
I didn't go to Paris. Not yet.
But maybe someday. Maybe when I'm ready.
I miss you more than any ocean can hold.
But today, I smiled without guilt.
And I think... you'd be proud.
I'll keep walking, my love.
Until we meet again.
Yours,
Ronak
The lantern lifted, flickering against the dark sky,
drifting out to sea.
He stood barefoot in the sand, his tears quiet now, his
heart still broken — but no longer empty.

THE DREAM THAT RETURNED

The rain returned to the city as if it had been waiting for Ronak — soft, persistent, and familiar. It draped the skyline in a melancholy haze, bringing memories with every drop. This was the kind of weather Tarini used to love. She'd dance barefoot on their rooftop, arms stretched, laughing like a child in defiance of sorrow.

Ronak stood by his window, watching the raindrops chase each other down the glass. The apartment still smelled like her — rose, sandalwood, and old books. He hadn't changed much since she left. He couldn't.

But something inside him had begun to shift.

For the first time in months, he had a dream.

And Tarini was in it.

In the dream, she wasn't sick. She wasn't weak. She wore a yellow kurta and her hair flowed with the wind. They were standing in a field of marigolds — endless gold stretching in all directions under a cotton-candy sky.

She smiled at him like she always did. That half-smile that made everything slow down.

"You kept your promise," she said, her voice softer than the breeze. "You carried me with you."

"I wasn't ready to let go," Ronak said. "I'm still not."

"You don't have to let go to move forward," she replied. "I never asked you to forget. Just to live."

And then she turned, slowly walking away into the marigolds, her silhouette fading into light.

Ronak woke with tears streaming down his cheeks — but his chest didn't feel like it was collapsing this time. For the first time, it felt... full.

He started sketching again.

It had been nearly a year since he last touched a canvas. But something about that dream stirred him awake. He bought new pencils, found his old sketchbook buried beneath dusty clothes, and began again.

His hands trembled at first. The lines were crooked, hesitant. But soon, the familiar rhythm returned. Lines turned to shapes, shapes to emotion.

The first drawing he completed was of Tarini — not from a photograph, but from memory. Her smiling in the rain, eyes closed, palms lifted to the sky.

He titled it: *Still Here.*

A few days later, Aisha visited again.

She had read his essay, watched his journey unfold online through the letters and shared posts. But seeing him now, sketching and sitting upright, she almost didn't recognize him.

"You look..." she paused, unsure. "Lighter."

Ronak nodded, a small smile appearing. "I dreamt of her. She told me to live."

Aisha's eyes welled up. She placed a wrapped parcel on his table. "There's something you should see."

Inside was a small printed booklet. The cover read:
Letters to the Moon — by Ronak.
He stared in disbelief. "You... published it?"
"Just a few copies. For now. People have been asking.
Your letters have helped them grieve, Ronak. You gave
them a voice when they couldn't find their own."
He ran his fingers over the cover. His name. Her legacy.
"I didn't do it for that," he whispered.
"I know," Aisha said gently. "That's why it matters."
The book launch was small. Intimate. Held at a local
bookstore, with fairy lights and tea and strangers who had
wept over words Ronak thought no one would ever read.
He stood before them, trembling, his voice cracking as
he read one of the final letters aloud.
Dear Tarini,
Today, they called me an author. But I'm still just a boy in
love with a girl who became the stars.
You're the reason I write. The reason I'm still here.
I carry your voice in every line.
I hope you hear it.
Always yours,
Ronak
There wasn't a dry eye in the room.
When he stepped down, people hugged him, thanked
him, handed him letters they had written to their own lost
loves. It wasn't just a book — it was a bridge between
hearts.
And Ronak felt, for the first time in what felt like
lifetimes, that he wasn't alone.
That night, back home, he lit a candle on the
windowsill.
No balloon this time. No letter.
Just the silence of a heart beginning to heal.

He opened Tarini's journal again and found a folded page he hadn't noticed before — written in blue ink, tucked between other notes.

If I'm not here one day, and you're reading this... I want you to know something.

You were my favorite story.

Every page, every second, every laugh, every tear — I wouldn't change a single thing.

Love is not about forever. It's about how deeply we can feel in the time we have.

And with you, I felt everything.

Ronak clutched the journal to his chest and cried — not with despair, but with gratitude.

She had loved him deeply.

And he had loved her fully.

And that was enough.

The next morning, he walked to the bookstore again.

A reader had left a letter for him. It was addressed simply: *To the one who writes to the moon.*

Inside, a young woman wrote about her sister, lost to illness. About how she read one of Ronak's letters and finally cried after years of holding it all in.

"Your words unlocked my grief. Thank you for letting love live even after goodbye."

Ronak closed the letter, looked up at the sky, and whispered:

"She's still changing lives, isn't she?"

And somewhere inside him, he swore he heard her voice again:

"Always."

CHAPTER FIFTY

HER ROOM IN THE SKY

Ronak hadn't been back to her home since the funeral. Her parents had invited him many times, gently, patiently, but he'd never found the strength. Every time he thought of walking through the gate, of seeing the place where she laughed, sang, slept — it felt like walking into a fire made of memories.

But now, nearly a year had passed.

The pain hadn't faded, not entirely. But something inside him was beginning to turn — not away from grief, but toward acceptance.

He stood in front of the familiar blue gate, hands trembling as he reached for the latch. It creaked open like a whisper from the past.

Tarini's mother greeted him with a quiet smile. Her eyes looked older, as if each day since Tarini's death had etched itself onto her skin. Yet there was still warmth in her embrace — the kind only a mother can give.

"I kept her room the way it was," she said softly. "I didn't know if that was right or wrong. I just... couldn't change it."

Ronak nodded. He understood.

Upstairs, the door to Tarini's room stood slightly ajar. He paused outside, taking a breath as though diving underwater, then pushed it open.

The room smelled the same.

Jasmine incense. The faint trace of vanilla lotion. And something else — something indefinable. Something that smelled like her laughter.

Her books still lined the shelves, most of them dog-eared and covered in post-it notes. Her handwriting danced in the margins: little jokes, ideas, scribbled hearts beside lines that made her feel too much.

Her bed was neatly made. A sketch he had given her — of the two of them under a tree — still hung on the wall beside the window.

It was like stepping into a memory that had refused to move on.

Ronak sat on her bed, running his fingers over the comforter, his eyes stinging as silence stretched thick around him.

On the bedside table, he noticed a box — simple, wooden, with his name carved on a small card taped to the top.

His breath caught.

He opened it slowly.

Inside were little fragments of her — and of them. A dried rose from their first real date. A movie stub. A shell from the beach trip they'd taken. A bracelet he had given her — woven by hand, imperfect.

Beneath all of it was a small sealed envelope.

His name, in her handwriting.

Ronak.

He opened it with reverent hands.

If you're reading this, it means I'm gone.
I'm sorry. I'm so sorry.
I wanted more time. With you. With the world. But mostly
with you.
You gave me the kind of love people write books about.
You were my calm in chaos. My constant. My dream.
And I need you to keep living.
Live loudly. Laugh shamelessly. Travel fearlessly. Love again,
one day — yes, even that.
Don't trap your soul in a story that ended. Write new
chapters.
But keep me in the footnotes, always.
Promise me something, okay?
When the sky turns orange — just for a moment — close your
eyes and say my name.
And I promise, I'll be there.
Still loving you,
Tarini

Ronak broke.

The tears came in heaving sobs, spilling from some locked chamber deep inside him. He held the letter to his chest and curled into her pillow, letting the weight of her absence fill every part of him.

But beneath the pain, a fragile thread of peace had started to form — a quiet acknowledgment that love like theirs didn't end. It changed. It lived on in letters, in sunrises, in every place he carried her memory.

Later that evening, as the sun began to dip below the horizon, Ronak stepped onto her balcony.

The sky burned orange and pink — the exact hue of the sunset they had once watched together from this very spot.

He closed his eyes.

"Tarini," he whispered.

And for a moment, the breeze curled gently around him. The wind played with his hair. A soft warmth bloomed in his chest.

She was there.

Not in body. Not in sound.

But in presence.

In peace.

On his way out, Tarini's mother stopped him.

"She always said," she began, her voice catching, "that you gave her a room in your heart. A permanent one. A place where she felt safe."

Ronak smiled softly. "She gave me one too."

He walked out of the gate with lighter steps than he'd entered, the box of memories clutched tightly in his hands.

That night, back at home, he sat down with his sketchbook.

This time, he didn't draw Tarini as she was in life.

He drew her in the sky — made of stars and clouds, surrounded by books, marigolds, paper lanterns, and letters.

He titled the page:

Her Room in the Sky.

And underneath it, he wrote:

This isn't goodbye.

It's just the space between our stories.

The Letters I Never Sent

Ronak had never been the kind of person who hoarded things. But when it came to Tarini, he couldn't throw anything away. Her handwriting on a grocery list. A napkin with a doodle. The old playlists she made for him on his phone.

They were anchors — small, fragile proofs that she had once lived and loved right beside him.

But after visiting her room, after reading that final letter, something had shifted. He still missed her every moment. Still dreamed of her voice.

But now, the pain wasn't only sharp. It was sacred.

That evening, he opened a new journal. One that had been lying untouched since the day of her cremation.

He wrote on the first page:

The Letters I Never Sent.

Dear Tarini,

It's been over a year. It still feels like yesterday. And forever ago.

Today, I laughed. A real, full laugh — the kind that surprises you. It scared me at first, like I was betraying you. But I remembered what you said — to live loudly.

I'm trying.

Some days, it still hurts like hell. Some nights, I cry so hard I can't breathe. But I've stopped hiding from it.

I think you'd be proud.

He kept writing.

Every day for the next two weeks, he'd write a new letter. Sometimes they were full of memories — like the first time she said she loved him, or the night they fought over pineapple on pizza and ended up dancing instead.

Other times, they were just raw confessions.

Dear Tarini,

I saw a girl today who had your hair. I followed her for three blocks, not like a creep, just... hoping. Isn't that ridiculous? Even after all this time, some part of me thinks maybe you'll come back. Maybe you'll walk in the door and tell me it was all just a test.

As the letters filled the pages, Ronak began to notice something. His sentences weren't always dripping in sorrow anymore. Some were light. Reflective. Even grateful.

Dear Tarini,

You taught me what love really is. Not the kind in movies. The kind that makes you want to be better. The kind that forgives, that stays even when it hurts.

You were my lesson. My gift. My heartbreak.

He decided to share one letter online — just one.

He picked one of the simpler ones. One that read:

Dear Tarini,

I made chai today. Spilled the milk, burnt the sugar, forgot the cardamom. You'd have laughed at me.

But I still drank it. Because it reminded me of you.

Love doesn't always need to be perfect. Sometimes it just

needs to be remembered.
– Ronak
He posted it late at night and didn't expect much.
By morning, it had gone viral.
Comments poured in.
Strangers from different cities, countries, languages —
sharing their grief, their own "Tarini," their own versions
of lost love. The comment that stayed with Ronak most
was:
"I never wrote to my mother after she passed. Your words
gave me permission."
He realized, then, that grief didn't isolate people.
Silence did.
But words... words connected.
One afternoon, Aisha showed up with a printer and a
mischievous grin.
"We're making another book," she said. "You don't get
a choice."
Ronak laughed. "I never do, do I?"
They called it: **"The Letters I Never Sent"** — a sequel,
but more than that, a bridge. Between pain and peace.
Between goodbye and memory.
The launch was bigger this time. But Ronak didn't cry
during his reading. Instead, he smiled as he spoke.
"Tarini once told me," he said, "that every person we
love carves out a room in our soul. Even after they're gone,
that room remains — sometimes messy, sometimes
painful. But always, always filled with light."
That night, after the event, Ronak stood on his balcony
and looked at the stars.
No letters. No balloons. Just silence.
And love.

A gentle wind brushed past him, and for a second, he could almost hear her laugh again.
He closed his eyes, smiled, and whispered:
"I'm still writing to you."
And in the quiet, he felt her answer — not in words, but in the warmth that lingered long after the wind had passed.

CHAPTER FIFTY-TWO

THE TEMPLE BELLS STILL RING

It was a Tuesday morning when Ronak found himself walking down the narrow lane that led to the small temple Tarini used to visit every month. He hadn't been there since she passed. Something about stepping into a space so soaked in her presence had always felt too overwhelming. But today, he didn't resist the urge. Today, he followed it.

The lane was just the same — small shops spilling spices onto the path, chaiwalas shouting at customers, and the faint hum of a bhajan playing from an old speaker perched on someone's windowsill.

The temple wasn't grand. It was a modest structure with peeling white paint, a marigold garland hanging from the arch, and the rhythmic clang of a bell echoing every few seconds. But to Tarini, it had always been sacred. She never came here for wishes or prayers. She came to *sit*. To feel silence. To just be.

Ronak slipped off his sandals and stepped inside.

The coolness of the marble beneath his feet made him pause. It was the kind of cold that calmed, not startled. A priest glanced at him, nodding gently, and returned to folding fresh flowers into garlands.

He walked toward the idol — the goddess draped in red and gold, her face serene and distant. Tarini used to light a small diya and then sit on the left side of the temple — always the left — where the morning sun cast a golden hue on the floor.

Ronak walked to that exact spot and sat down.

The air smelled of incense and wet stone.

And suddenly, the stillness wasn't empty — it was *full*.

Full of everything unspoken. Every conversation they never had. Every word they couldn't fit into their short forever.

His fingers trembled slightly as he took out the small notebook from his pocket — the one he'd been carrying around since he started writing the letters.

But this time, he didn't write.

He just looked at the pages.

The ink. The tears smudged into them. The memory of her laughter tucked between the lines.

She was still here.

Maybe not in the way he wanted.

But in a way that mattered.

As he sat there, a little girl came and sat beside him. Her hair was tied in two braids, and she was humming a tune softly.

"You're sad," she said, looking at him with the kind of blunt honesty only children possessed.

Ronak chuckled, surprised. "Yeah. I am."

"Someone you love went to the stars?"

He nodded. "How did you know?"

She pointed up. "That's where my papa went. I talk to him every night."

Ronak looked at her, heart aching. "Does it help?"

She smiled, big and innocent. "Yes. Because I know he hears me. Even if I don't hear back."

Then she stood, bowed slightly toward the goddess, and skipped away, her anklets jingling with every step.

He sat for a while longer, letting the moment settle around him like soft dust.

As he finally got up and walked out, he turned back to look at the temple bells swinging gently in the wind.

They hadn't stopped ringing.

Not since Tarini had left.

Not even once.

He realized then — grief doesn't silence the world. It only sharpens the sounds you notice. It teaches you to hear the echoes, the whispers, the bells that still ring after the music has ended.

Outside the temple, he bought a small marigold garland — the kind Tarini used to hang on her room's window hook every time she felt hopeful.

Back at home, he placed it on his desk, just beside her last letter.

Then he sat down, opened his notebook, and finally wrote again:

Dear Tarini,

I went to your temple today. The bells are still ringing.

I think they always will.

And now, instead of hurting... they comfort me.

Maybe healing isn't forgetting.

Maybe it's remembering, with less ache and more love.

Yours, always,

Ronak

CHAPTER FIFTY-THREE

Her Voice in the Rain

The rain came without warning that afternoon.
It wasn't the usual summer downpour — it was gentler, quieter. The kind that whispered rather than roared. Ronak stood by the window of his apartment, watching droplets gather on the glass, blurring the view of the city skyline beyond.
Tarini had loved the rain.
She would run out barefoot at the first sign of it, arms wide open, face tilted to the sky. He used to tease her, calling her "baarish ki deewani" — a rain fanatic. But truthfully, he had adored her even more in those moments — so wild, so free, so alive.
And now, whenever it rained, he didn't hide from it.
He let it soak him with memories.
Today, as the storm grew outside, Ronak did something he hadn't done in months. He opened the folder on his laptop named "Tarini's Voice Notes."
It had only a few files. She hadn't liked recording things, always saying that living in the moment was better than storing it. But once, during a particularly long work

trip of his, she had sent him a few messages — small monologues, random thoughts, even silly jokes.

He clicked on one.

Her voice filled the room.

"Hi love, I know you're probably buried in your laptop, being all serious. But guess what? It rained today. I went out to the terrace — barefoot, of course — and thought of you. Do you remember the first rain we shared? You called me crazy. But I saw you smiling when you thought I wasn't looking…"

He closed his eyes, letting her words wash over him.

"Anyway, I hope it rains there too, so we can feel the same sky. I miss you. Come back soon. I love you more than I can ever explain."

He didn't realize he was crying until a tear hit the keyboard.

It wasn't the first time he'd listened to her, but today, it felt different. It didn't shatter him. It didn't send him spiraling into a pit of longing.

It warmed him.

Like the rain on her terrace.

Later that evening, the power flickered and went out. The apartment fell into soft darkness, lit only by the occasional lightning flash and the steady sound of rain.

He lit a candle — not because he needed the light, but because she would've.

Tarini always lit candles during storms. "It makes everything feel softer," she'd said once, nestling beside him under a blanket.

Ronak sat near the balcony door, watching the world blur.

And suddenly, on impulse, he stepped out.

The rain kissed his skin like a memory.

It wasn't cold. It wasn't harsh. It was like her —
persistent, quiet, comforting.

He stood there, face to the sky, eyes closed, arms
hanging at his sides. And in the rhythm of the rain, he
heard her voice again — not from a recording, but from
somewhere deeper.

**"Live, Ronak. Even if it hurts. Especially when it
hurts."**

He laughed.

It came out of nowhere. A single, startled laugh. Then
another. And before he knew it, he was grinning like a
fool, soaked to the bone, laughing and crying at once.

Because even in death, Tarini hadn't left.

She was still here — in the rain, in the wind, in the
flicker of candlelight and the echo of her old voice notes.

He whispered, "I miss you."

And somewhere in the thunder, he felt her whisper
back.

"I know."

When he finally came inside, drenched and shivering,
he grabbed a towel and sat on the floor of the living room,
the candle still flickering nearby.

He opened his notebook and wrote:

Dear Tarini,

It rained today. The kind of rain you'd have danced in.

*I listened to your old messages. You didn't just record your
voice — you captured moments. Feelings. Love.*

You're still teaching me things.

*You always said that grief wasn't meant to trap us, but to
shape us.*

Today, I believe you a little more.

Love,

Ronak

He closed the notebook and looked out the window
once more.
The rain had slowed.
But inside him, something had begun again.

CHAPTER FIFTY-FOUR

SHADOWS AND LIGHT

The days were growing shorter, the air cooler, but Ronak felt the weight inside him as heavy as ever. It was a strange kind of heaviness—one that settled in your chest and refused to leave, no matter how deeply you breathed.

He had started avoiding the places they once loved to go, fearing the sharp edges of memory would cut too deep. But today, something inside him demanded otherwise.

He found himself walking towards the old park where he and Tarini had spent countless evenings. The rustling leaves whispered stories of laughter and quiet confessions. The bench where she had rested her head on his shoulder was still there, a little worn, touched by time but unchanged.

Sitting down, Ronak closed his eyes and tried to imagine her sitting beside him—the warmth of her presence, her gentle breath, the softness of her hand in his. But all he could feel was the cold breeze teasing his skin, reminding him she was gone.

Yet, within that coldness, he noticed something else—a faint warmth, like the first shy light of dawn breaking through the darkness.

He opened his eyes to see the sun piercing through the clouds, casting golden patches on the damp grass. The light and shadows danced together, just like their memories—sometimes bright, sometimes dark, but always intertwined.

A small child ran past him, laughing and chasing after a butterfly. The carefree joy in the child's eyes made Ronak smile. Maybe this was what Tarini had meant when she told him to live even when it hurt. To find light amidst the shadows.

He pulled out his notebook and began to write:
"Dear Tarini, today I sat where we once sat together. The world still moves, still breathes, even without you. I see shadows in every corner, but I also see light breaking through. I think I'm learning to live with both."

As he wrote, a woman approached, holding a flower in her hand. She smiled kindly and sat at the other end of the bench.

"Beautiful day," she said softly.

"Yes," Ronak replied, returning her smile.

For a few moments, they sat in comfortable silence. Then she spoke again, "Sometimes, the hardest part is learning to carry the memories without letting them weigh us down."

Ronak looked at her, surprised at how much those words resonated. "Yes. It's like shadows and light... they both live inside us now."

She nodded. "Exactly. And in that balance, we find peace."

Ronak felt a small spark of hope flicker inside him. Maybe, just maybe, the pain would soften with time. Maybe the shadows wouldn't consume him, because the light would always be waiting.

As the sun dipped lower, Ronak stood up. Before leaving, he placed a small stone on the bench—a quiet tribute to the love that had shaped him.

Walking away, he whispered into the fading light, "Thank you, Tarini, for teaching me to see the light, even when all I wanted was to be in the dark."

CHAPTER FIFTY-FIVE

THE QUIET ROOM

Ronak hadn't visited the hospital in weeks. Not since the day Tarini was admitted, the day that had shattered everything and rebuilt it in grief. Yet, today, something pulled him there—a whisper of unfinished business, a thread he couldn't let go.

The sterile smell greeted him as he entered, mingled with the faint hum of machines and distant footsteps. He walked past the reception, nodding at familiar faces, until he reached the corridor that led to the quiet room—the place where Tarini had spent her last days.

He paused outside the door, heart heavy, hands trembling. The room looked just as it had the last time he saw her—white walls, a simple bed, a chair by the window. But now, it felt emptier, colder.

Ronak stepped inside and sat on the edge of the bed, the mattress still holding the shape of her. He traced an invisible path where her hand had rested, fingers intertwined with his.

He closed his eyes and took a deep breath.

The silence was almost unbearable.

And yet, within that silence, he heard something else—the faint echo of her laughter, the soft murmur of her voice, the way she used to whisper his name when the world felt too dark.

"Tarini..." he whispered, "I'm here."

He reached into his pocket and pulled out a folded letter, one he had written but never sent.

My love,

I don't know how to say goodbye when you're still in every part of me. The world feels different without you—quieter, colder, less bright. But I carry you with me. In every breath, every heartbeat.

I promise to live, not just exist. To find moments of joy, even when the pain is raw. To remember your smile, your kindness, your light.

This isn't the end for us. You're in me—in my memories, in my dreams, in the spaces between the stars.

Forever yours,

Ronak

He unfolded the letter carefully and laid it on the bedside table. Then, with a shaky hand, he touched the small bouquet of flowers Tarini's mother had left behind—fragrant jasmine mixed with marigolds.

For a long time, Ronak sat there, letting the quiet room hold his grief and his love. It was the last place they had been together, but it was also the place where he would begin to heal.

Before leaving, he stood by the window and looked out at the world beyond—the same world Tarini had dreamed of, full of possibilities and light.

He whispered one last time, "I love you, Tarini. Always."

And stepped into the waiting day, carrying her memory like a gentle flame.

CHAPTER FIFTY-SIX

WHAT REMAINS IN DUST

Ronak stood at the edge of the riverbank, the water flowing endlessly beneath the bridge, as if carrying away every sorrow it touched. The sun was setting, painting the sky in hues of orange and pink — colors Tarini had loved.

He clutched a small box tightly in his hands. Inside it was a delicate silver chain, a gift Tarini had once given him on their first anniversary. He had kept it hidden since the day she passed, afraid to wear it, afraid to face the flood of memories it would bring.

But today, he wanted to honor a promise — the promise he had whispered to her in the quiet room.

"To live."

With a deep breath, Ronak opened the box. The chain shimmered softly in the fading light. He slipped it around his neck, feeling the weight of it settle against his chest.

A tear escaped his eye, tracing a path down his cheek.

"I'm still here, Tarini. Still holding on."

He knelt by the water and took a small handful of pebbles. One by one, he tossed them into the river, watching the ripples spread wide.

"Each one is a memory," he murmured. "Each one a moment we shared. I'm letting them go, but I'm not forgetting."

The river carried the stones away, just as time carried his grief. But the love — the love was his anchor, the unbreakable tether that kept him grounded.

Behind him, the world moved on. Children laughed in the distance, couples walked hand in hand, and the city's heartbeat pulsed steadily.

Ronak smiled faintly. Maybe Tarini was there too — in the laughter, the warmth, the endless sky.

He stood and faced the horizon, feeling the promise echo inside him.

No matter what, he would live. For her. For himself. For the love that never truly dies.

CHAPTER FIFTY-SEVEN

TALKING TO THE DEAD

The evening had settled like a soft blanket over the city. Ronak sat alone in his small living room, the dim light of a single lamp casting long shadows across the walls. Silence filled the space, but it was not peaceful—it was heavy, like a thick fog pressing down on his chest.

He reached out and picked up Tarini's favorite book from the coffee table. The edges were worn, the pages yellowed from countless readings. She had always loved losing herself in stories, but now, every word felt like a reminder of the emptiness she had left behind.

He flipped through the pages slowly, searching for a line she had once marked with a delicate finger. The passage was about love and loss, about holding on and letting go. Ronak's breath caught as he read it aloud in a whisper:

"To love is to risk pain, and to lose is to know the depths of the heart."

He closed the book and rested it on his lap. The weight of silence was suffocating, but it was also a mirror to the void inside him.

Memories flooded back—Tarini's laughter, her touch, the way her eyes sparkled when she talked about dreams. How could something so beautiful end so painfully?

The phone buzzed on the table, breaking the silence. Ronak glanced at the screen. It was a message from Tarini's mother: *"We are coming over tonight. You don't have to be alone."*

A small, grateful smile softened Ronak's features. Even in the darkest moments, the threads of connection remained—fragile but real.

He typed back a quick reply, then leaned back in his chair, closing his eyes.

The silence remained, but now it felt different—less like a weight, more like a space waiting to be filled. Filled with memories, with love, with the promise of healing.

For the first time in a long time, Ronak allowed himself to breathe freely.

He knew the road ahead would be long and uncertain.

But he also knew he wasn't walking it alone.

And maybe, just maybe, that was enough to start again.

CHAPTER FIFTY-EIGHT

THE LIGHT IN THE WINDOW

The night was quiet except for the distant hum of the city and the occasional flicker of headlights passing by. Ronak sat near the window, watching the soft glow of a streetlamp outside cast long shadows on the floor. The room felt colder without Tarini's laughter filling the air, without her gentle presence making the house feel like home.

His fingers traced the rim of a cup of tea he hadn't yet touched, as if grounding himself through the simple gesture. The night stretched endlessly, wrapping around him like a heavy cloak. He closed his eyes and let memories flood in — the way Tarini's eyes sparkled with mischief, the softness of her voice when she whispered his name, the warmth of her hand in his.

There was a knock at the door. Startled, Ronak stood and opened it to find his childhood friend, Aanya, standing there with a small, hesitant smile.

"I thought you might need company," she said softly, stepping inside.

Ronak nodded, grateful for her presence. She sat down beside him, her hand reaching out to gently rest on his arm. It was a simple touch, but it spoke volumes—a reminder that even in loss, connection remained.

Together, they looked out the window at the night sky. The stars were faint but steady, like silent witnesses to his grief and resilience.

Aanya broke the silence. "I know it's hard. But there's still light, Ronak. Even when it feels like everything has gone dark."

He swallowed hard, the lump in his throat growing heavier. "I keep waiting to see her—just one more time. But all I see is empty space."

She squeezed his arm gently. "She's there. Not in the space, but in the light. In the love you shared. In every breath you take."

Ronak took a deep breath and looked again at the soft glow outside. For the first time in a long time, it didn't feel distant. It felt like hope—a fragile, flickering flame, but light nonetheless.

He whispered, "I miss you, Tarini."

And in the quiet room, under the watchful stars, he felt her presence — a light in the window, guiding him home.

CHAPTER FIFTY-NINE

GRIEF IS A HOUSE

Ronak sat at his desk, surrounded by scattered photographs and scraps of paper. Each image held a fragment of their life together — moments frozen in time, smiles captured forever, tears unspoken. It was like piecing together a broken mirror, hoping the shards would reflect something whole again.

He carefully picked up a photo of Tarini laughing under the monsoon rain, her hair drenched, eyes sparkling with joy. The memory behind it was vivid: that day, they had danced in the streets, drenched but alive, unaware that time would be so cruel.

He traced the outline of her face with a trembling finger, feeling the ache sharpen.

The room was quiet except for the soft rustle of pages turning. Ronak opened a notebook—one where he had poured out his heart in letters he never sent. His handwriting wavered, but the words held raw honesty.

"Tarini, I don't know how to live without you. The silence around me is deafening, and yet I hear your voice in every corner of this house. How do I hold onto the fragments without falling apart?"

A tear slid down his cheek as he folded the page gently and placed it back.

He stood and walked to the window, looking out at the city's endless pulse. Life went on — laughter, chatter, footsteps — but his world felt paused, suspended between what was and what could never be again.

His phone buzzed. A message from Aanya: *"You don't have to do this alone."*

Ronak smiled faintly, grateful for her steady presence. Maybe healing wasn't about fixing everything at once. Maybe it was about gathering fragments, one by one, and learning to live with the cracks.

He picked up the photo again and whispered, "We're still here, Tarini. In every broken piece, in every memory."

And with that, he allowed himself to hope — that even fragments could create a mosaic of love

CHAPTER SIXTY

A New Dawn

The first light of dawn crept gently through the curtains, casting a soft glow over the room. Ronak sat by the window, his eyes tracing the horizon where the sky met the earth, painted in shades of pink and gold. The world was waking up, and with it, a fragile hope stirred inside him.

It had been months since Tarini's passing, yet the ache in his heart remained. Grief was no longer a sharp wound but a quiet companion, lingering in every breath and every silence. Still, today felt different—like the moment between night and day when everything is possible.

He reached into his pocket and pulled out the silver chain Tarini had given him. The one he had worn every day since her last goodbye. He touched it gently, feeling its cool weight, a reminder of a promise made—a promise to live.

His phone buzzed softly. A message from Aanya: *"Let's take that trip we talked about. For you, for her."*

Ronak smiled faintly, the idea of moving forward no longer seemed impossible.

He stood, stretched, and looked around the room that held so many memories—some joyful, some painful. It was time to make new ones.

As he stepped outside, the cool morning air filled his lungs. The city was alive with possibility—the chatter of early risers, the smell of fresh bread from a nearby bakery, the soft rustle of leaves in the breeze.

Ronak took a deep breath and whispered to the wind, "This one's for you, Tarini."

With each step, he felt the weight of sorrow lift just a little. The road ahead was uncertain, but for the first time in a long time, he was ready to walk it.

A new dawn was breaking—not just outside, but inside him too.

And with it came the promise of healing, of hope, of love that never truly fades

CHAPTER SIXTY-ONE

SHE'S STILL EVERYWHERE

The afternoon sun filtered through the half-open curtains, casting soft golden patterns on the floor. Ronak sat alone in his living room, a book resting unopened in his lap. His eyes, however, were distant, staring past the familiar walls and into a place only he could see—a place where memories of Tarini still lived.

It had been nearly a year since that cruel day when the world seemed to stop spinning. Since Tarini's laughter was silenced, since the warmth of her hand was no longer in his. The pain had not dulled; it had transformed—becoming a quiet ache, a persistent echo in the chambers of his heart.

Sometimes, when the house was silent, Ronak thought he could still hear her voice, soft and clear, calling his name. He would close his eyes, willing himself to believe for just a moment that she was near. But when he opened them, the emptiness pressed in again, heavier than ever.

He reached for the small box on the table beside him—the one filled with letters Tarini had written but never sent. She had always been a writer, a dreamer, her words weaving emotions he often struggled to put into sentences. Ronak unfolded one carefully, the paper fragile beneath his fingers.

"Ronak, if you are reading this, it means I am no longer with you in this world. But I want you to know, my love for you is eternal. You are my strength, my home. Live for us both. Find happiness again, even if it feels impossible now."

His throat tightened. The letter was her final gift, a piece of her soul left behind. He pressed it to his chest, closing his eyes as tears slipped down his cheeks.

"Tarini," he whispered, "how do I move on when every part of me is still yours?"

The room grew quiet except for the ticking of the clock on the wall—a relentless reminder that time marched forward, indifferent to grief.

Ronak stood and walked to the window, looking out at the city buzzing with life. People hurried past, wrapped in their own stories, unaware of the battle raging inside him.

But in that moment, something shifted. The ache in his chest was still there, but beneath it was a flicker—a fragile, hesitant spark of something else.

He remembered a night not long after Tarini's death, when he had stood alone under the stars, feeling utterly lost. And then, as if from nowhere, a shooting star had streaked across the sky. He had closed his eyes and wished—wished for strength, for healing, for the courage to keep living.

Maybe that wish was beginning to come true.

Ronak took a deep breath, feeling the weight of grief mixed with the lightness of hope.

He opened the letter again and smiled softly. "I'll try, Tarini. For you, for me."

The echoes of her love reverberated through his soul, reminding him that even in loss, connection remained. That though she was gone, the heart never truly forgets. And as the sun dipped lower, casting long shadows across the room, Ronak felt a quiet peace settle over him—a promise that the journey ahead, though difficult, was not one he had to face alone.

THE LETTERS I BURNED

The evening sky was painted with hues of orange and purple, the sun slowly descending beyond the horizon. Ronak sat on the worn-out bench in the park where he and Tarini had spent countless afternoons. The scent of blooming jasmine floated in the air, a bittersweet reminder of the days when life had seemed so full of promise.

The bench felt colder without her beside him. He reached into his pocket and pulled out a small, folded note—one of the many she had slipped into his hands during their time together. The edges were worn, and the ink slightly smudged, but the words still held the same warmth.

"Even when I'm not with you, I'll be your shadow—always near, always watching over you."

Ronak clutched the note tightly, his fingers trembling. The weight of memories was heavy, pressing down on his chest like an invisible force. Each memory was a double-edged sword: a source of comfort and pain intertwined.

He remembered the day they first met, under the golden light of a late afternoon. Tarini had been sitting alone, lost in a book, her smile radiant when he had shyly approached. That moment had sparked a flame neither expected to burn so brightly.

And how they had promised to face the world together, come what may.

But life had other plans.

He wiped away a tear as his mind wandered to the last time he saw her. The hospital room had been sterile and cold, so unlike the warmth she always carried. Yet, even in her frailty, Tarini had held his hand and smiled—a smile that was brave, tender, and full of love.

"Don't carry this grief alone," she had whispered, her voice barely audible. "Live for both of us, Ronak."

Those words haunted him. How could he live when a part of him felt hollow, missing the very soul that had completed him?

Ronak looked around the park. Children played, couples walked hand in hand, and old friends chatted on nearby benches. Life moved forward, indifferent to his sorrow.

But as the sky darkened, he felt a strange calm settle over him. Perhaps it was the way the stars began to twinkle—a silent promise that even in darkness, light could be found.

He pulled out his phone and opened the gallery. Pictures of Tarini smiled back at him—her laughter frozen in time, the sparkle in her eyes, the gentle tilt of her head when she looked at him. Each photo was a fragment of a love story that death had tried to erase but could never truly destroy.

Ronak whispered, "You're still here, aren't you? In every memory, in every heartbeat."

The breeze carried the soft rustle of leaves, as if the world itself was responding to his plea.

He took a deep breath, feeling the weight of memories shift—not as a burden, but as a legacy. A reminder of a love that had changed him, shaped him, and would live on through him.

For Tarini, for their dreams, and for the promise of a new dawn, Ronak stood up. He folded the note carefully and slipped it back into his pocket.

The path ahead was uncertain, the pain real. But so was the strength he carried within—the strength born from love, loss, and the courage to keep moving forward.

With one last look at the fading sky, Ronak whispered, "I will carry you with me, always."

And as the night embraced the city, a quiet hope blossomed in his heart—a hope that one day, the weight of memories would become the wings that set him free.

CHAPTER SIXTY-THREE

SILENT PROMISES

The early morning light spilled softly across Ronak's room, casting long shadows that danced on the walls like ghosts of the past. The silence was thick, broken only by the faint ticking of the clock and the distant chirping of birds waking to a new day. Ronak lay still on his bed, staring at the ceiling, lost in the weight of thoughts that seemed too heavy to carry.

Tarini's absence echoed in every corner of the house—the empty chair at the dining table, the untouched cups of tea she used to make, the worn-out book she never got to finish. The world had changed so much since that final moment, but in some ways, it felt frozen in time—trapped in the memory of her smile, her laughter, her touch.

He closed his eyes and saw her face—soft and radiant, framed by strands of hair that caught the morning light. That image had been etched into his heart forever, a silent promise that no distance, no death, could ever erase.

Ronak sighed deeply, the air heavy with unspoken words and broken dreams.

He reached out and touched the photo frame on his bedside table. It was the one from their last anniversary—him and Tarini, wrapped in a tight embrace, eyes full of hope and love. He whispered, "I miss you, Tarini. Every day, every moment."

The pain was a dull ache now, not as raw as before but persistent, a constant reminder of what was lost. But beneath the sorrow was a determination—a vow to honor her memory, to live the life she had wished for him, even when it seemed impossible.

The room was filled with memories—small tokens of their life together. A scarf she had knitted, a playlist of songs they loved, letters she had written but never sent. Each one was a piece of her, a thread connecting the past to the present.

Ronak sat up and reached for a letter she had left on his desk. The handwriting was familiar, looping gracefully across the page.

"My dear Ronak, if you are reading this, it means I am watching over you from afar. Life is fragile, and sometimes cruel, but love is the thread that holds us together. Promise me you'll find joy again, even if it takes time. Promise me you'll keep dreaming, keep living."

His eyes blurred with tears, but he smiled—a small, bittersweet smile. He folded the letter carefully and tucked it into his pocket.

Outside, the city was awakening. The hum of life stirred—the honking of cars, footsteps on pavements, voices greeting the morning. Ronak felt the pull of the world beyond his walls, a call to step forward, to embrace the uncertain future.

He stood and walked to the window, looking out at the bustling streets below. Somewhere out there, life continued, full of new stories, new beginnings. He wanted to be part of that again, but the path was tangled with memories, with shadows of the past.

Yet, in the quiet of the morning, a fragile hope took root. He could almost hear Tarini's voice whispering, encouraging him to be brave, to keep moving despite the pain.

Ronak took a deep breath, feeling the weight on his chest lighten just a little.

He made a silent promise—to live for both of them, to carry her love in his heart, to find meaning in the days ahead.

As the sun climbed higher, bathing the room in warm light, Ronak knew the journey was far from over. But for the first time in a long while, he felt ready to take the next step.

With a steady heart and silent promises, he opened the door and stepped into the new day.

CHAPTER SIXTY-FOUR

DEATH DIDN'T WIN

The rain tapped softly against the windowpane, a rhythmic whisper that matched the slow beating of Ronak's heart. He sat by the window in the quiet room, wrapped in a thick shawl Tarini had knitted for him last winter. The fragrance of wet earth mixed with the faint scent of her perfume lingering in the air—an invisible thread tying him to the past.

Outside, the world was blurred in shades of gray, but inside, memories blossomed vividly—each one a fragment of the life they had shared. He closed his eyes and saw her smile, bright and unguarded, lighting up even the darkest moments. Her laughter echoed like music in his ears, reminding him of the joy they had once known.

But those fragments were shards now—beautiful yet sharp, cutting through his soul whenever he reached for them.

He opened his eyes and gazed at the small wooden box on the table, filled with mementos: photographs, pressed flowers, ticket stubs from movies, and tiny notes folded with care. Each piece told a story, a chapter of their love that no one else would understand as deeply as he did.

Ronak carefully lifted a photograph—a candid shot of Tarini, her hair tousled by the wind, eyes shining with mischief. It was taken during their trip to the hills, a place they had promised to return to together. But fate had stolen that promise away.

He traced the outline of her face with his finger, feeling the cold glass beneath his skin. "Why did you have to leave so soon?" he whispered, voice breaking.

The room felt heavy with absence, yet filled with the presence of a love that refused to fade.

He remembered the countless nights they had spent planning their future—dreaming of a small home filled with laughter, of children's footsteps echoing through the halls, of growing old side by side. Those dreams now felt like distant stars, shining but unreachable.

But Ronak held onto them still, because to let go completely would be to forget her entirely—and that was a pain greater than any grief.

He reached for a letter Tarini had written during one of her hospital stays. Her handwriting was faint, but her words carried strength and hope.

"Ronak, my love, even if my body fails me, my heart beats for you always. Don't let my absence dim your light. Carry our memories like a flame, and let it guide you through the darkest nights."

Tears welled up as he read the letter again, feeling the warmth of her spirit infuse his being.

Outside, the rain began to soften, turning into a gentle drizzle. Ronak rose and moved to the door, stepping out into the cool air. The world was quiet, wrapped in a peaceful stillness that contrasted the storm within him.

He wandered down the familiar streets, each step stirring a memory—a cafe where they had shared coffee and secrets, the bookstore where she had picked out novels for him, the park where they had carved their initials into the bark of an old tree.

All these fragments of 'us' were scattered around him, waiting to be gathered and cherished.

Ronak knelt beside the tree and ran his hand over the initials, faded but enduring.

"Tarini," he murmured, "I carry you with me—in every breath, every heartbeat. You are the part of me that will never break."

A soft breeze stirred the leaves above, as if the world itself was answering him.

He stood and continued walking, feeling lighter somehow. The fragments of their love, though painful, were also his strength. They were proof that what they had shared was real, timeless, and worth holding onto.

And as the clouds began to part, letting the sun peek through, Ronak smiled through his tears. The past was a part of him, but so was the future—and he would face it with Tarini's memory lighting the way.

CHAPTER SIXTY-FIVE

I Still See Her

The room was quiet except for the steady, rhythmic beep of the heart monitor—a sound that had become both a comfort and a torment to Ronak. He sat by the bedside, holding Tarini's frail hand in his own, the warmth slowly fading but the bond between them as strong as ever.

Outside, the monsoon rains poured down in sheets, as if the sky itself wept for the inevitable. The gray clouds hid the sun, mirroring the heaviness in Ronak's heart. He hadn't left her side in days, refusing to let go even when her breaths grew shallow and her eyes fluttered with pain.

"Tarini," he whispered, voice cracking with unshed tears, "please stay with me. Just a little longer."

She opened her eyes weakly, and for a moment, recognition flickered in their depths. A faint smile touched her lips—a smile that was both a farewell and a promise.

Ronak bent closer, brushing a stray lock of hair from her forehead. "I'm here," he said, swallowing the lump in his throat. "Always."

Time seemed to slow as memories flooded his mind—moments of laughter beneath starry skies, stolen glances filled with unspoken love, the warmth of her hand in his during times of despair. Each memory was a fragile thread connecting their souls, a tapestry woven with joy and pain.

He remembered the day they first met, how her smile had shattered the loneliness he didn't know he carried. How their dreams had intertwined like vines, promising a lifetime together.

But life's cruel twist had shattered those dreams, leaving him with fragments of a love that was now slipping away.

Tears escaped and traced silent paths down his cheeks.

"I'm sorry," he whispered. "I couldn't save you."

Her fingers tightened just slightly around his—a tiny spark of life, a fragile connection refusing to break.

"Don't be," she murmured softly, her voice barely audible. "You gave me everything... love, hope, strength. That's more than anyone could ever ask."

Ronak's heart ached, torn between hope and despair. He wanted to hold on, to believe in a miracle, but the truth was undeniable. Tarini's light was fading.

He leaned his forehead against hers, drawing comfort from the warmth that still lingered.

"Promise me," she said faintly, "promise me you'll live. Not just survive—live, truly live."

His breath hitched. "How can I, without you?"

She smiled weakly, eyes filled with a love so deep it transcended pain. "Because I'll always be with you—in your heart, in your memories. I'll be your strength when you feel weak."

Ronak nodded, tears flowing freely now. "I promise."

The heart monitor beeped steadily as her eyelids fluttered one last time. Her hand slipped from his, resting gently on the white sheets.

"No," Ronak cried, clutching her hand desperately. "Stay with me, Tarini."

But the world was silent except for the steady beep, now slowing, a heartbreaking rhythm of farewell.

She was gone.

The room felt emptier than ever, the air thick with loss. Ronak sat back, his body trembling as the weight of grief crashed over him like a tidal wave. The love of his life, his everything, was no longer there.

Yet, amid the heartbreak, a quiet resolve grew inside him.

He whispered into the stillness, "Goodbye, my love. Thank you for every moment."

Days passed like a blur. Friends and family offered condolences, but Ronak felt alone in a sea of sympathy. His grief was a solitary journey, one that no words could soothe.

But slowly, something began to change.

He found himself revisiting the places they had loved—the park bench where they had dreamed aloud, the café where she had ordered his favorite chai, the hilltop where they had watched sunsets together.

Each place was a sanctuary, a place where Tarini's spirit lingered like a gentle breeze.

Ronak started writing again—letters to her, stories of their love, poems that spilled from his soul. Writing became his way to keep her alive, to transform pain into something beautiful.

One evening, as the sky blazed with the colors of dusk, Ronak stood by the river where they had first met. He released a small lantern into the flowing water, watching as it drifted away, carrying his love and sorrow into the horizon.

"I'll live, Tarini," he vowed quietly. "For you, for us."
Though the wound in his heart remained, so did the
love—a love that death could not erase.
And in that love, Ronak found the courage to face the
future, carrying her memory like a flame that would never
be extinguished.

CHAPTER SIXTY-SIX

QUIET BEGINNINGS

The first light of dawn crept cautiously over the city skyline, spilling muted shades of pink and orange across the horizon. The air was crisp and cool, holding the lingering scent of night rain and jasmine from the nearby gardens. As Ronak stepped out of his apartment, the morning seemed to hold its breath — still, tender, expectant.

His feet touched the cracked pavement with a hesitant rhythm. Each step was a small rebellion against the weight that had anchored him for so long — a silent vow that today, he would try to move forward, even if only an inch.

The streets were quieter than usual, a soft hush cloaking the city as it shifted from night's deep stillness toward the hum of waking life. The first chirps of sparrows flitting through rustling branches filled the air, mingling with the distant clatter of shutters being raised and the muted murmur of early risers.

Ronak breathed deeply, letting the cool, fresh air fill his lungs, trying to anchor himself in the present. The world around him was vibrant — yet somehow, it felt both familiar and new, as though seen through the fragile lens of someone just beginning to heal.

He walked slowly toward the corner where Raju's tea stall stood — a modest wooden cart nestled beneath a large neem tree. Raju himself was already there, sweeping the small area with practiced care, his face creased by a thousand smiles and sorrows. When Ronak approached, the old man's eyes brightened with genuine warmth.

"Good morning, Ronak bhai," Raju greeted, his voice gravelly but kind. "A cup of chai to start your day?"

Ronak nodded, offering a faint smile that surprised even him. The simple act of ordering tea felt like a small ritual of normalcy, an anchor in the drifting sea of his thoughts.

As Raju prepared the chai — boiling water, fragrant masala spices, rich milk, and a generous spoon of sugar — Ronak watched the steam rise, curling and twisting into the morning light. The aroma was intoxicatingly familiar: sweet, spicy, and warm, promising comfort in a cup.

He accepted the cup with both hands, letting the warmth seep into his fingers. Taking a slow sip, he closed his eyes, allowing the complex flavors to unfold — cardamom, ginger, cinnamon — a symphony that spoke of home and belonging.

Sitting on a nearby bench beneath the neem's broad canopy, Ronak let his thoughts drift. The memories of Tarini settled softly, no longer sharp pangs but like gentle echoes.

He recalled mornings much like this — sunlight filtering through curtains, the sound of her laughter as she brewed tea, the soft touch of her hand on his arm. Each recollection was a precious thread woven into the fabric of his being, unbroken by time or loss.

Feeling the urge to capture his swirling emotions, Ronak pulled his journal from his bag. The leather cover was worn and supple, the pages inviting and blank. He found a quiet spot in the shade, the dappled sunlight playing through the leaves above, and opened to a fresh page.

His pen hovered for a moment before beginning to write, the words flowing slowly, deliberately:

"Today feels like the first page of a new chapter — fragile, uncertain, but alive with possibility. The pain has not left me, but it no longer consumes every breath. There is space here now for something else: hope, perhaps, or the courage to try."

"The city breathes around me, pulsing with life. I want to be a part of that again — not as a ghost drifting through shadows, but as someone who still belongs, still feels, still dreams."

As the sun climbed higher, the city began to stir more vividly. Vendors opened their stalls, the scent of fresh bread and ripe mangoes mingling in the air. Children's laughter rang out as they hurried toward school, their backpacks bouncing against their backs. Old men played chess under banyan trees, their quiet murmurs punctuated by the clack of pieces on boards.

Ronak walked slowly through the streets, absorbing the vibrant tapestry of life around him. Every sight, sound, and scent was a reminder that the world was still turning — that there was still room in it for him.

He found himself wandering toward a small park, where flowering bougainvillea spilled over iron fences, painting the air in brilliant reds and pinks. The scent was intoxicating, mingling with the earthiness of freshly turned soil and the faint trace of rain still clinging to leaves.

Beneath a spreading banyan tree, he sat on a weathered bench, tracing the rough bark with his fingertips. The tree's ancient roots twisted and knotted into the earth like silent sentinels — symbols of endurance and quiet strength.

Here, away from the noise of the city, Ronak allowed his tears to fall. They were not tears of despair, but of release — a cleansing rain washing away the grief that had shackled him for so long.

As the afternoon sun warmed his skin, Ronak felt a fragile shift within himself. The journey of healing was far from over, but in this moment, beneath the banyan's embrace, he glimpsed a path forward.

He closed his journal, sliding the pen into his pocket. Rising slowly, he looked up at the sky — now a deep blue, flecked with drifting clouds. The light was different now, softer and more forgiving.

On his way back, he passed a small bookstore — a cozy haven of worn shelves and whispered stories. It was a place Tarini had loved, a place where time slowed and words held magic.

Drawn inside, Ronak ran his fingers along the spines of books, feeling the weight of stories waiting to be told. He picked up a slim volume of poetry, its pages yellowed with age, and settled into a corner to read.

The verses spoke of love, loss, and the quiet resilience of the human heart — of how even in the darkest nights, dawn eventually breaks.

Evening fell softly, casting a golden glow over the city. Ronak returned home, carrying with him a new sense of purpose — fragile but real. Lighting the candle on his desk, he sat down to write one last entry in his journal:

"This day was the first step on a long road. I do not know what lies ahead, but I am no longer afraid to walk into the unknown. The memories of Tarini will always be with me — not as chains, but as wings."

As he lay down to sleep, the city hummed quietly beneath a blanket of stars. The pain was still there, but so was a fragile hope — a promise whispered by the dawn's first light.

And for the first time in a long while, Ronak felt ready to meet the new day.

PART III

The Unfinished Story

CHAPTER SIXTY-SEVEN

A DISTURBING DISCOVERY

The sterile smell of antiseptic hung thick in the air of the hospital corridor. Ronak's footsteps echoed faintly as he made his way past nurses and doctors moving briskly, their faces worn from long shifts but indifferent to his silent turmoil. The hospital felt cold—an unforgiving place that had once cradled Tarini's final moments, and now, held the shadows of unanswered questions.

He clutched a worn file in his hands, the edges frayed from being opened and closed countless times. His eyes scanned the official documents with painstaking attention, searching for any detail that might have slipped past before.

The medical report described the cause of death as blunt trauma to the head, consistent with a fall down the staircase in their apartment building. An accident. The police investigation had concluded the same, closing the case within days. But the bruise on her wrist — that small, inexplicable mark — pulled at something inside him, refusing to be ignored.

He stared at the page again and again: a faint, irregular bruise, darker at the edges, as if inflicted by a deliberate grip rather than a random scrape.

His fingers traced the line slowly, as if by touching it, he could feel the truth hidden beneath the paper. His mind raced, piecing together what little he remembered from the days before Tarini's death.

Memories flooded in—snapshots of laughter turning into silence, whispered conversations suddenly cut short, the way Tarini's eyes had clouded with fear during their last week together. She had seemed restless, distracted — like she was carrying a secret too heavy to share.

He had asked her, gently, but she always smiled and brushed it off, saying it was just stress, work pressures. Now, that smile felt like a lie.

Ronak's breath caught in his throat. If Tarini had been afraid, if someone had hurt her — then who? And why?

His thoughts were interrupted by the soft murmur of footsteps approaching. A nurse passed by, glancing at Ronak with a brief look of sympathy. She didn't speak, but something in her eyes told him he wasn't the first to search for answers here.

Feeling a sudden surge of urgency, Ronak stood and walked to the nurses' station. The young woman behind the desk looked up, startled by his sudden presence.

"I'm sorry to bother you," he said quietly, voice steady despite the turmoil inside. "I need access to the CCTV footage from the apartment building on the night of Tarini's death."

Her eyes widened. "That footage was sealed as evidence. Only the police and court have access."

Ronak swallowed hard. "Please... I have to know what really happened. Tarini wasn't just... It wasn't an accident."

The nurse hesitated, glancing toward a supervisor down the hall. After a tense moment, she leaned in and whispered, "There have been rumors... things people noticed but never reported. You're not the only one doubting the story."

Hope flickered in Ronak's chest, mingling with fear. "What kind of rumors?"

Before she could answer, her supervisor appeared and gently steered her away. Ronak was left standing there, alone with his questions.

Back outside, the afternoon sun felt harsh on his skin as he walked slowly down the street. The city's noise seemed distant, like a world he no longer belonged to. But the bruise, the rumors — they were clues, fragments of a puzzle he was determined to solve.

He pulled out his phone and called an old friend — a private investigator named Arjun, someone he trusted implicitly.

"Arjun," Ronak said as soon as the call connected, "I think Tarini's death wasn't an accident. I need your help."

There was a pause. Then, a steady voice replied, "I'll come by tonight. We'll figure this out."

As Ronak ended the call, a cold wind swept past him, carrying with it the echo of a question he couldn't shake: Who had wanted Tarini gone?

And would finding the answer put him in danger, too?

To Be Continued In:

**"FADING INTO FOREVER: What Remains
After Truth"
Book II of the Fading Series.**

✦ Thank You For Reading ✦

To the one holding this book in your hands or scrolling through its final pages — thank you.
You didn't just read a story. You carried it, felt it, and gave it life. You walked beside Ronak as he mourned, as he searched, as he broke and tried to rebuild. You held Tarini's memory in your heart even after she left. And in doing so, you've honored what this book was meant to be: a reflection of love, loss, grief, and the quiet courage it takes to keep going.
This isn't just a fictional journey. It is a mirror of every silent goodbye, every memory we hold in the dark, every unanswered question that lingers when someone we love is taken too soon.
If it made you cry — thank you for feeling.
If it made you question — thank you for thinking.
If it stayed with you — thank you for letting it.

♡ What Comes Next ♡

The story doesn't end here.
Ronak believed he knew how Tarini died. But buried beneath her goodbye are truths even more painful than loss.
A voicemail left unsent. A photo that shouldn't exist. A name spoken in fear. And a shadow that's been following him since the night everything changed.
She didn't just die. She was silenced.
And someone will do anything to keep that silence unbroken.
The story continues in Book Two: Fading Into Forever: What Remains After Truth
Coming Soon
Get ready to step into the aftermath — where love turns into vengeance, and justice becomes the only way to say goodbye.

✦ A Note From The Author ✦

Fading Into Forever was not born from just imagination. It came from real emotions, from the parts of myself I don't often show. Writing this book meant opening wounds I thought had healed, exploring the what-ifs I usually run from, and sitting with characters who taught me more about being human than most real-life conversations ever have.

Ronak's grief is the grief we carry long after funerals end. Tarini's courage is the quiet strength so many possess but never get recognized for. And their love — no matter how short-lived — is a reminder that even the smallest spark can light up the darkest chapters of our lives.

This book taught me that it's okay not to have all the answers. That endings aren't always neat. And that sometimes, the most powerful stories are the ones that leave us aching for what comes next.

To everyone who has loved deeply, lost tragically, and still finds the courage to hope — this story is yours

.Hrishikesh Karmakar.

♡ Stay Connected ♡

The end of a book is never really the end — not for the characters, and not for the ones who loved them.
If you've made it this far, you're not just a reader. You're a part of this journey. You've lived through Ronak's pain, Tarini's silence, the haunting beauty of their love, and the unanswered questions left behind. And as this chapter closes, I want to invite you into the next one — not just in fiction, but in real connection.
I didn't write Fading Into Forever just to tell a story. I wrote it to start a conversation. About grief. About love. About letting go and not knowing how. About the strange way our lives keep moving forward even when it feels like everything we loved has stayed behind. And you — the reader — are the reason those conversations matter.
If this book touched you in any way — if you found a piece of yourself in its pages, if you're still holding Tarini in your heart, or if you're just wondering what happens next — I would love for you to stay in touch.
Here's how:
? Join the Mailing List
hrishikeshkaraam96@gmail.com

Get early updates about the sequel, exclusive bonus scenes, deleted chapters, and behind-the-scenes thoughts from my writing desk. I promise not to flood your inbox — just quiet notes from a storyteller to those who listen.
? Follow on Social Media
Instagram-hrishi__karm
Let's continue the conversation. I share raw writing moments, inspirations, emotional quotes, and updates

about future releases. More importantly, I love hearing from readers — your reactions, your theories, your favorite lines. Don't be a stranger.

? Use the Hashtag: #FadingIntoForever
If you post a photo, quote, or thought about the book, use the hashtag. I keep a close eye on it, and I read everything. Truly. Your reflections matter more than you know.
?? Write to Me
Yes, really. I read every message. Whether you want to share how the book moved you or just say hello, you can reach me directly via the contact form on my website or through direct messages.
We are all just stories in the end.
But the best stories are the ones we carry together.
Let's carry this one a little further.
With love and gratitude,
Hrishikesh Karmakar

✦ If You Loved This Book... ✦

Please consider leaving a review if this story found a place in your heart, I would be deeply honored to hear your thoughts. Every word, every emotion woven into these pages was written with love, and knowing it resonated with you means the world to me. Please mention me on Instagram @hrishi__karm and share your experience or even a heartfelt rating. Your words are more than just feedback—they're a connection, a reminder that stories truly live on in the
hearts of those who feel them.

♡ A Thank You Letter To You — My Reader ♡

Dear Reader,

As I sit here trying to find the right words, I realize there may never be enough to express what I truly feel. But I will try — because you deserve them.

Thank you.

Thank you for choosing to pick up Fading Into Forever. Thank you for giving Ronak and Tarini a place in your heart, even if only for a few pages. Thank you for walking beside them — through their joy, their silence, their heartbreak, and their unraveling truths.

This story was never meant to be easy. It was written with pain, grief, love, and longing stitched into every chapter. There were nights I cried writing it. Mornings I questioned if I had the strength to keep going. But I did — because I believed someone out there needed this story the same way I did. Maybe that someone was you.

To everyone who's ever lost someone too soon...

To everyone who's ever wondered what more they could have done...

To everyone who still loves in the silence — you are not alone.

You carried this story through to the end. And in doing so, you've become part of something that lives far beyond the final page. Every tear you shed, every sentence you reread, every moment you paused just to breathe — it means more to me than you'll ever know.

This is not just my story.

It's ours now.

And though Tarini's voice has gone quiet, and Ronak's path has turned darker, this is not the end. Their journey continues — and if you're willing to walk with them once more, I promise: the truth will change everything.

Until then, thank you.

From the depths of my heart, thank you for believing in love — even the kind that hurts.

With all my gratitude,

Hrishikesh Karmakar

Author of Fading Into Forever

✦ Final Goodbye ✦

If you've reached this page...
You are proof that stories can bring hearts together —
across time, space, language, and grief.
Whether you cried, questioned, or simply felt
something, thank you.
I hope this book left you with more than heartbreak.
I hope it left you with reflection. With meaning. With
something that lingers.
Because that's what love does.
It lingers, even when the person is gone.
Just like Tarini.
Until next time,
Hrishikesh Karmakar...
♡♡♡